(Biggie, Mary J. Blige, Lil Wayne, and Chuck D) . . . George's tightly packaged mystery pivots on a believable conspiracy . . . and his street cred shines in his descriptions of Harlem and Brownsville's mean streets." —*Library Journal*

"George is a well-known, respected hip-hop chronicler . . . Now he adds crime fiction to his resume with a carefully plotted crime novel peopled by believable characters and real-life hip-hop personalities." —*Booklist*

"George's prose sparkles with an effortless humanity, bringing his characters to life in a way that seems true and beautiful." —*Shelf Awareness*

"Part procedural murder mystery, part conspiracy-theory manifesto, Nelson George's *The Plot Against Hip Hop* reads like the PTSD fever dream of a renegade who's done several tours of duty in the trenches . . . *Plot*'s combination of record-biz knowledge and ghetto fabulosity could have been written only by venerable music journalist Nelson George, who knows his hip-hop history . . . The writing is as New York as 'Empire State of Mind,' and D is a detective compelling enough to anchor a series." —*Time Out New York*

"A breakbeat detective story . . . George invents as much as he curates, as outlandish conspiracy theories clash with real-life figures. But what makes the book such a fascinating read is its simultaneous strict adherence to hip-hop's archetypes and tropes while candidly acknowledging the absurdity of the music's current big-business era. There's a late-capitalism logic at work here. If this book had been written in the early '90s, it would have been about the insurgent artistry of hip-hop musicians and the social-justice strides the genre was effecting. Today, it's a procedural about the death of principles." —*Time Out Chicago*

"*The Plot Against Hip Hop* is a quick-moving murder mystery that educates its audience on Hip Hop's pioneer generation along the way . . . it is a nostalgic look at a magical and manic moment in time." —*New York Journal of Books*

"George very masterfully has created a novel that informs as well as entertains." —*Huffington Post*

"A welcome nostalgic trip." —*Chicago Tribune*

"Nelson George comes from an older generation that still remembers Hip Hop as the vital and dangerous voice it once was. This feeling for the past carries throughout the novel, and manages to convey the weight and importance of this profound shift in values without being nostalgic . . . *The Plot Against Hip Hop* is a fine piece of 'edutainment'—both exciting and thought provoking . . . it's great to finally have a novel about Hip Hop written by one of [its] original documentary journalists." —*ABORT Magazine*

"One of our coolest cultural critics has written a mystery page-turner about the underbelly of hip hop, and it's woven with signature whip-smart insights into music. Nelson George's smooth security-guard-turned-detective, a.k.a. D, scours a demimonde as glamorous as Chandler's Los Angeles. This plot has more twists and turns than a pole dancer, and D definitely needs an encore—he's destined to become a classic." —**Mary Karr, author of** *The Liars' Club*

for *The Accidental Hunter*

"Great reading for the criminal-minded" —*Vibe*

"The most accomplished black music critic of his generation." —*Washington Post Book World*

"There are few people who can put the past seventy years of urban reality into the perspective of the most recent hip minute like Nelson George. He braids actual facts and fictional characters flawlessly." —**Chuck D, Public Enemy**

"George is an ace at interlacing the real dramas of the world . . ." —*Kirkus Reviews*

"George is a well-known, respected hip-hop chronicler . . . Now he adds crime fiction to his resume." —*Booklist*

Nelson George is an author, filmmaker, and lifelong resident of Brooklyn. His books include the first four novels in his D Hunter mystery series: *The Accidental Hunter, The Plot Against Hip Hop, The Lost Treasures of R&B,* and *To Funk and Die in LA.* Among his many nonfiction works are *The Death of Rhythm & Blues, Hip Hop America,* and *The Hippest Trip in America: Soul Train and the Evolution of Culture & Style.* As a filmmaker he has directed the documentaries *Brooklyn Boheme, Finding the Funk,* and *A Ballerina's Tale.* He was also a writer/producer on the Netflix series *The Get Down.*

THE
Darkest Hearts

THE
Darkest
Hearts

A D Hunter Mystery

NELSON GEORGE

BROOKLYN, NEW YORK

Published by Akashic Books
©2020 Nelson George

Hardcover ISBN-13: 978-1-61775-822-5
Trade Paperback ISBN-13: 978-1-61775-809-6
Library of Congress Control Number: 2019943605

Akashic Books
Brooklyn, New York
Twitter: @AkashicBooks
Facebook: AkashicBooks
E-mail: info@akashicbooks.com
Website: www.akashicbooks.com

To the real Edgecomb Lenox
and his friends

If it is impossible to stop, then we must lead it and direct it.
—Russian president Vladimir Putin on rap music in his country,
December 15, 2018

Like any good earth-spanning tale, hip hop started with truth, evolved into myth, and degenerated into a moneymaking enterprise. Along the way its roots were viewed as a discovery, an origin story, an oft-told tale, and then just that blah-blah-blah thing you've heard too many times.

The myth outlived the truth (as it tends to), the details grew fuzzy (even to those who lived it), and eventually it all gave way to cliché.

But the enterprise of hip hop lives on like Frankenstein's monster, constantly updated, remixed, repackaged, rebranded, and rebooted, until all that is left is a series of craftily commodified gestures of rebellion. Such is the way of culture in the United States, a rapacious and gluttonous land where progress is a market-driven code word and technology a heedless gateway to obsoleteness. There are no real gatekeepers in America, only salesmen for whom this year's model is next year's landfill.

So citizens of this republic of all colors and creeds, being Americans, took this cultural expression and squeezed it until it bled green. All manner of sex, love, fetish, stereotype, spirituality, dance, and rhythm could be poured into a glass of commerce like juice from a lemon. Let's bring that bitter drink to our lips and taste what it has become.

—Excerpt from the unpublished manuscript of *The Plot Against Hip Hop* by Dwayne Robinson (2011)

CHAPTER ONE
SICKO MODE

D Hunter sat in a Cadillac Escalade rolling down Forsyth Street SW in Atlanta. He was sitting behind a man named Ant and studying the roll of fat on the back of the guy's clean-shaven head. D thought this man desperately needed to change his diet. He had no idea if Ant was any good in his roles as road manager and bodyguard, but he was absolutely sure Ant had spent too many nights eating at a local Waffle House.

"Turn that shit up!"

The man who requested the increase in volume was the rising MC Lil Daye, a lean, handsome young black man in his early twenties who sat next to D, wearing a vintage Atlanta Braves baseball cap, Gucci shades, a $50,000 ring, and a $65,000 bracelet. He was also puffing chronic; acrid smoke curled around D's nose like cooked cabbage.

The driver, an older black man by the name of Sammy (a cousin of Lil Daye's mother), turned up the volume on "Slip Slippin'," a joint with a jittery beat that shook the SUV like the Batman ride at Six Flags. D felt his body inadvertently moving to the beat; his better judgment and old-school taste bulldozed by the volume.

"You feel it, huh?" said Lil Daye.

D laughed and admitted, "I guess my body can't help it."

"Yup, pardner," the MC laughed, "that's why I fucks with you."

Lil Daye was a prime purveyor of trap, a music that had made the hip hop D had grown up with a twenty-first-century museum piece. Beats sampled from vinyl recordings had largely been replaced by digital files and "original" music, a.k.a. skittery, slithery, jiggling rhythms found in computer programs, sounding like C-3PO on E. Trap shouted, *The future is now!* The electronic farts and bleeps of today were the fat bass lines of the past.

The gift of polyrhythmic delight, splendid syncopation, and complex wordplay that once delighted D had given way to lyrical repetition, fuzzy enunciation, and narrowly defined experience. There were scores of trap rappers who thought older microphone techniques were for middle-aged dinosaurs. Trap music sounded to D like punk rock must have sounded to Marvin Gaye fans in 1977: amateur, limited, unintelligible, and offensive.

Yet there D was, sharing a ride with Lil Daye, heading to a strip club in ATL, and deeply in business with the paragon of the music that had killed his old gods. Atlanta was the official center of twenty-first-century hip hop and had essentially held that title since the late nineties. New York was the foundation, Los Angeles was the expansion, and Atlanta was the evolution.

A former Atlanta mayor had represented local MCs on his rise to power. Ludacris had his own damn holiday weekend here. Whether you were born in NOLA or New York, if you were serious about hip hop now, you had a McMansion in DeKalb County. As parties in the park had been to the Bronx and swap meets had been to Los Angeles, strip clubs were ground zero for hip hop in Atlanta, because this was where hits were certified, legends created, and aspirations fulfilled. The cassette mixtape was dead. Big butts in clear heels were eternal.

"I got you tonight, D," Lil Daye said when they arrived. "It's all on me, pardner."

Pardner wasn't a regular part of Lil Daye's vocab, but the twenty-three-year-old performer was being literal tonight. Earlier in the day, D had closed a lucrative deal between Facebook, his own management company, and Lil Daye's Yung Culture. The trap star would create original content for Facebook Watch, using the ginormous platform to promote his new music. R'Kaydia Lelilia Jenkins, who ran Future Life Communications, a company that specialized in hologram technology, had helped D broker the deal with the aid of his longtime adviser and silent partner, Walter Gibbs.

D and R'Kaydia's relationship had as many ups and downs as a brightly lit yo-yo. It was a business relationship with a charged sexual subtext that neither openly acknowledged. But at the end of the day, she was a black businesswoman who enjoyed the chess of the white-boy tech game, and D had an uncanny way of dealing with mercurial musicians. (His years as a bodyguard, musician, and archivist always came in handy.) Gibbs had been a friend and occasional business adviser since the days when D ran a club-security concern in NYC. Now they were both LA-based expats whose Big Apple relevance had faded.

There was no sexual subtext at Magic City; sex is the *text* of every strip club. Capitalism, fetishism, dominance and submission, erectile dysfunction, lesbian erotica, and bisexuality all fill in the subtext quite nicely. But to D, strip clubs were only about one thing—loneliness. He'd never been to one that wasn't populated by sad-eyed, slack-jawed, robotic men who used greenbacks and mechanized dancers to fake real human connection. It was also a site for contempt. He thought some dancers hid it well, but it was the coin of the realm for the women who looked down at their customers and saw graves behind their eyeballs. Strip clubs, for all their flashing lights, booming sound systems, and bodacious backsides, were mortuaries where true intimacy was embalmed.

As he, Daye, D, and Ant slid behind a VIP table, D wondered what it said about his love life that he'd agreed to a night in this emotional sinkhole. His thoughts flowed back to loves won and lost.

There was Emily, his mixed Brit chick from the turn of the century, who was now a mother but still hosted old-school hip hop jams in Manhattan. There was Michelle Pak, his Korean almost–great love, who was building a business in South LA and, according to Instagram, had just spent a ski weekend in Aspen with some all-American white man.

The saddest memory of all was Amina Warren-Jones, whose memory haunted even when he was happy. She was brown, lean, and had the loveliest voice that had ever whispered in his ear. Amina had been murdered because D had unearthed a crazy plot against hip hop and sought out its architects, one of whom was her ex-husband. D had her death avenged, but that act of violence brought no closure, no resolution, no satisfaction. Amina was dead and part of D had gone to the grave with her. She'd been poisoned with the HIV virus. D hadn't infected her but the means of her demise had been devised to exploit his weakness.

These days D's T cell count was almost normal and his health was Magic Johnson remarkable. His HIV infection was not gone but was in a surprising middle-aged slumber. He still took his meds, but only in small doses, and sometimes forgot them for days at a time. D had outlived the plague years but the psychological damage, while muted, could still be felt. Revealing his status was not something he did easily. The words *I am HIV positive* made him feel guilty. To the world, D was a broad-backed African American man who favored black clothes that matched his ferocious game face. Inside, D was a small, fragile soul who couldn't stand to see the fear in the faces of prospective lovers whenever he told on himself.

D truly knew the deadness of the strip club since, for a time, he'd been addicted to its cosmetic eroticism. He had fallen for the brightly colored dance floors and the booming music. He'd indulged in this substitute for intimacy so deeply that he'd come to hate himself and the falsehood the whole enterprise was predicated on.

When D pulled himself out of his own head and looked over at Lil Daye, he noticed that his new partner was not looking up at the dancers spinning and twirling in the vicinity. He was FaceTiming a woman. Lil Daye, like many MCs, had a steady woman and kids in a roomy ATL suburb. D hadn't met them, but from the pictures in Lil Daye's office and on social media, he seemed to be a doting daddy with his little boy, at least when he wasn't talking about trap houses, sports, and haters on the mic. His wife, known as Mama Daye, was a large, fleshy woman who'd built a substantial social media following by giving fashion and grooming tips to big-boned women. Lil Daye had mentioned getting her on a reality show, which was something D would work on back in Cali.

Like any good pop star, Lil Daye was a mythmaker and shape-shifter. The distance between his real life and his surreal persona was a map more complex than any of his fans could have drawn. So when Dorita Johnson showed up at Magic City, D had to make some new calculations.

Dorita wore very little makeup on her honey-colored face, though her lip gloss did pop. Wearing ripped black jeans, fluffy mules, and a black tee with Lil Jon looking manic on the front, she was dressed conservatively (as far as strip club attire goes). She was clearly fit, with broad shoulders, a tapered waist, and legs that were no strangers to lunges. Her hair was cut into a black bob, kind of a young Halle Berry meets Toni Braxton look, which was a major contrast to the weave-centric hairstyles of the strippers and waitresses at Magic City. D knew that in Atlanta, strip clubs had been so normalized that couples went there on dates and straight women could be found there after work for drinks. Still, Dorita had a casual, unpretentious vibe that threw off D's radar. She could have been an off-duty cop or a white-collar worker with a bit of after-work style.

But wherever Dorita worked, it was obvious when she kissed Lil Daye and snuggled up next to him that their relationship was happily unprofessional. D was introduced as "the new business pardner I told you about," a clue that this was not just a jump-off but someone Lil Daye confided in. Dorita surveyed D quickly, politely shook his hand, and then turned her attention back to the rapper. The two lovers whispered to each other, oblivious to the music, the lights, and the dancers. They may have been in a citadel of false intimacy, but these two resided in a lovestruck world.

D just smiled and nodded when Lil Daye leaned over and said, "I gotta step. Whatever you want here is on me. See you tomorrow." Then he exited with Dorita, while Ant moved into the seat next to D. For Lil Daye, this strip club visit was just a pretext for a romantic rendezvous, but Ant apparently had something he wanted to say. It was the first time they'd been alone since D arrived in Atlanta.

"So," D asked, taking the initiative, "are we cool, Ant?"

"Pardner," Ant replied with a sarcastic tone, "far as I'm concerned, you got nothing to worry about as long you deliver those bags for Lil Daye. Do your job and me and you are good. I'll leave it like that right there."

"Looking forward to working with you, Ant."

Ant nodded goodbye and placed a small stack of singles in front of D, which somehow felt like a dis.

D stayed another fifteen minutes before ordering an Uber to go to the Four Seasons in Midtown.

That Lil Daye was a cheater was no surprise. That his mistress was an attractive, normal woman, and not a pole goddess, was. It made Lil Daye much more interesting, D thought, though now having to keep his secret was irritating.

When he stepped outside Magic City his cell rang. Unknown number. As a general rule, D didn't answer blocked numbers. He figured if he didn't have their number, it meant he didn't know them and may not want to. But it had been an evening with an unexpected twist so D decided to see where this call would take him.

"This is Ice," the voice said.

Hearing the sandpaper voice sent a chill through D like it was January in Chicago. "It's been awhile," D said.

He hadn't spoken to Ice in several years, not since the ex-gang-banger and hit man had avoided incarceration in a case involving corrupt Brooklyn detectives and real estate speculation in gentrifying neighborhoods. But the connection between D and Ice was deeper than that. It was Ice, with D's nodding approval, who'd eliminated one of the men behind that plot against hip hop. D didn't know all the details since Eric Mayer's body had never been found.

"I know you're in Atlanta," Ice said. "So am I."

"You live here now?"

Ice ignored the question. "We need to meet. Something has come up."

CHAPTER TWO
BACK TO BLACK

The Landmark Diner on Roswell Road was idyllically old school and all-American. Its signage was iridescent neon—its reds almost pink, its blues almost aqua. The big clock above the doorway was a predigital-era throwback.

It had the long horizontal design typical of 1950s dining. Next to the windows were booths with Formica tables and aqua-colored seats. The Landmark had weathered Atlanta's headlong rush into modernity by fetishizing the Eisenhower years.

Of course in that decade, one much beloved by both godless plutocrats and working-class Christians, the idea of two black men sitting for a late-night chat at the Landmark would have been impossible unless they were in the back sharing Newports and washing dishes. These days the Landmark was a nonsmoking establishment. So instead of cigarettes, the two men shared a plate of fries doused in ketchup, which Ice was supplementing with a strawberry milkshake. The drink left a little pale ring around the mouth of Ice's otherwise dark-chocolate face.

Back in crack-era Brownsville, a Brooklyn hood filled with public housing, welfare recipients, and poverty-stricken families, Ice had been a fearsome legend. He'd been a real-world boogeyman and a brutal role model. He'd emerged from the Jolly Stompers (an eighties youth gang that spawned "Iron" Mike Tyson) and blossomed into a fearsome contract killer: tall, wispy thin, and as adept with handguns as he had once been with a basketball. Word in the Ville was that Ice could have easily gotten an athletic scholarship and, with some weight training, made the NBA.

Ice's family was food-stamp poor so he chose fast, short money over potential long green. First it was just robbing drug dealers—busting into fortified apartments, snatching girlfriends and sisters as bargaining chips, digging strongboxes out of public housing concrete. One robbery had gone badly and he had to shoot a dealer; the man bled out.

Word spread that Ice was fearless, and an offer came his way for $10k to go up to the Bronx and put a bullet in the head of a man just back from upstate. For a day, Ice had wrestled with the ethics of it. That first killing had happened in the heat of the moment, but this job was to be done in the coldest of blood.

Well, Ice went to the Bronx and did the job. Then another. Then another. To justify this new profession, Ice decided to view people as a farmer did. Some animals were food. Either they died or you died. Some animals were milked and their product could feed you or be sold. You stayed alive when they did. This way people, like animals, existed to either feed you or make you money.

This allowed Ice to ignore the reality that these dead human beings had all been a black or brown man just trying to feed their family outside the "official" economy. Ice had spent a lot of his days *not* acknowledging that he was what Public Enemy called a real-life "antinigger machine."

Ice was a grown man now. What he'd done at sixteen and seventeen could not be undone. Over time, Ice had owned a video arcade (back when that was a viable ghetto business), financed several barbershops, and would hit off promising young people who needed cash for clothes or computers. If the god his mother prayed to on Sundays really did exist, Ice hoped he'd balanced the books enough to reserve a room in hell's coolest condo.

Another bargaining chip with God was that Ice had given D a crucial tip back when D was mourning the murder of his mentor, the critic and historian Dwayne Robinson.

D had first encountered Robinson at the door of New York nightclubs where his old company, D Security, protected entrances and dance floors. Eventually, D read Robinson's magnum opus, *The Relentless Beat*, a huge history of black music in America. Backstage at an LL Cool J concert, D peppered Robinson with questions about the text. Impressed by D's interest, Robinson took the big man to lunch and a friendship grew out of that conversation. Robinson loved the backstage gossip D had access to, while D found his growing understanding of music history an asset in dealing with clients.

When Robinson was stabbed to death on a SoHo side street by two members of the Bloods, D was devastated. He didn't believe this was some random act of violence. That suspicion was bolstered by the theft of *The Plot Against Hip Hop*, the manuscript for Robinson's next book. This began an investigation which became a crusade, where rogue FBI agents and messianic businessmen conspired to use money, surveillance, and psychology to manipulate hip hop. Eventually, the coconspirators became rivals, creating a subterranean version of the East Coast/West Coast rap battles of the nineties.

Two of Ice's protégés had been used as hit men in Robinson's death, which is how D and Ice first met, forming an uneasy alliance that resulted in the termination of Eric Mayer in a Canarsie basement (or so D surmised). A few years later, when Ice was implicated in another murder, it was D who kept him out of harm's way.

So now they sat across from each other in the brightly lit Georgia diner, far from Brooklyn, each in debt to the other, an awkward truth that the taste of late-night fries didn't disguise. Back then, Ice had been bald with a diamond in one earlobe and a thin goatee. The man sitting across from D had a thick salt-and-pepper beard, black-rimmed nerd glasses, and teeth as yellow as cheddar cheese. Moreover, his body was seriously filled out. No longer light-pole lean, today's Ice had bulked-up shoulders and spread across the waist. Whether it was because of age or the additional weight, Ice looked like a former lightweight who'd moved up several weight classes. You could mistake him for a different man if you ignored his eyes which, despite the glasses, were still as cold as winter on an elevated subway platform.

D said, "You didn't answer when I asked if you're now living in Atlanta."

Ice looked at D like this was a very silly line of conversation. "I'm here now, right? You are here too, but I understand you out in Cali now. So we are where we are."

D tried again for a human connection: "My grandfather died."

"Got shot I heard." Ice wasn't about to get all warm and fuzzy.

"Yes."

"Damn," Ice said, "you Hunters got a real thing going on with God."

"Or the other guy maybe."

This made the man crack his ice grill a bit. "I dunno. I knew your brothers Matty and Rashid a little bit. As far as shit goes, they weren't into anything real deep. Bullets do lie. Believe that. I know."

"I do too," D said. "So, how bad is our situation?"

"Two weeks ago some people went fishing off Canarsie Pier. Hooked a motherfucking arm. Now, motherfuckers been dropping bodies off Canarsie Pier since the Jews ran Murder Incorporated in the Ville. The Italians took over Canarsie and dropped more bodies there than Joe

Pesci in *Goodfellas*. But the arm they found belonged to Eric Mayer. I ain't no scientist so I don't know the process, but I know the result."

D absorbed this mix of history and unwelcome information, then asked if Ice had a plan of action.

"Well," Ice said, "the easiest thing to do would be for all concerned parties to just shut the fuck up."

Ice hadn't said this like a threat. His voice was bone dry. But the words sent a serious chill up D's spine. When confronting fear, D had always felt it best to address it head-on. He said, "Or eliminate the other concerned parties?"

Ice laughed. "Yo, if this was '95 and we was back in BK, I guess it could go down. But it ain't and we aren't, so take a breath and unclench your butt cheeks." After that, Ice took a big sip of his milkshake and sat back.

D said, "You know Mayer was an ex-FBI agent?"

Ice's eyes got wide and then small again, like a cat about to sleep. He looked out the window as if all the cars in the parking lot were suspect. Finally he said, "All I knew for sure was that he was a gunrunner and that he'd pulled some of my crew into some stupid shit and that he was getting in my way."

"Here's the thing: he and another ex-agent were running wild all up in hip hop. Thought they were the second and third coming of Suge Knight." D leaned toward Ice and lowered his voice. "He'll be just another cold case in the Ville—lots of those, right?" He was looking for reassurance, but that wasn't how Ice got down.

"Well, someone's been asking about him," Ice said. "That's why I know about the arm. Wasn't NYPD but maybe some FBI version of internal affairs, now that you tell me this. I'm sure they'll have questions since it's one of their own."

"Have they been asking about you?"

Now Ice was smiling again; he enjoyed being notorious. "Nigga, you know they're always asking about me. When a body pops up in Kings County, the first thing they do is wonder if Ice did it. I'm the easy answer to every lazy cop's question."

"What happened to those two kids?"

Something approaching softness crossed the hit man's face. "Tracy is dead, remember?"

"Oh yeah," D said, feeling like a fool.

"He died doing something stupid," Ice said. "The other one is all right. Doing good." This moment of sentimentality passed as quickly as it came. "You doing business in ATL now, huh? You fuckin' with Lil Daye, right?"

"I just made him a big deal. I'm doing management now, not security."

"Huh. Good for you. You know much about his man, Ant?"

This caught D off guard. "If you're asking, then probably not enough."

"ATL is full of opportunity. Ambitious motherfuckers with good old country hustle. But if you're from out of town, you probably don't know the story behind the story. Watch Ant."

"He a problem?" D asked.

"Were you a problem when you were a bodyguard?"

"A bit."

"Well, he's a *real* problem, not a toy one like you."

"You are full of good news tonight, Ice."

"Nigga, it's never a good look when I show up." Ice finished off his milkshake. "You done all right for yourself. Got better clothes. A tan. A better business that you can use your brain for and not your body. It's a good look. A long way from the Tilden projects. But know this: at some point you may have to decide what you need to do to keep it. Nothing gives more sleepless nights than keeping the past in the past."

"Could it really get bad for me?"

Ice leaned across the table. "Yo, you see who's president, right? Well, a black man these days who ain't prepared for the worst? He ain't been paying attention."

CHAPTER THREE
WICKED GAMES

From the sky, the streetlights below were intersecting strings of pearls. Red pearls moved in staccato unison. The white pearls were static, but given the illusion of movement by the plane's descent. Every few minutes, a string of green pearls appeared, but that just seemed a tease, like a green-eyed stranger who glanced your way one afternoon and never looked back.

It could have been any city anywhere. Red lights. White lights. Green lights. Long rows of them bunched together like children over tables of free ice cream. Serene Powers had seen a lot of them in the past several years—these twenty-first-century cities that were unique in name only.

Fast-food jobs. Revitalized downtowns. Homeless people. Shattered civility. Incipient fascism. Serene remembered Detroit and its seven blocks of branded vitality, while homeless people huddled in the dark by the bus depot. That was an extreme case, but it fit the overall pattern. Every city. Every town. Condo corridors with construction cranes, welcoming more. She remembered Seattle with cranes decorated with green lights hovering above the skyline like metallic trees.

Serene wondered if she were exaggerating. So much travel. So much ugliness. Was she too jaded now to feel a city's individual swagger, or to smell its aroma? Perhaps she had gone over that edge where her visual perception was totally dulled. She searched her memories of this weird occupation she'd taken on, and all she recalled were strings of red, white, and green pearls.

London, she hoped, would be different. It was her first assignment outside of North America. It was an old modern city, which meant it would have all the old and new vices. Serene wanted London to surprise her, but she was sure it wouldn't. The doors she had to open in London were the same doors she would find anywhere else: doors to the personal hell of the poor, the desperate, the gullible. Hello, London. Hello, world.

A few hours later, Serene soaked in a big bathtub at a hotel on Soho's Dean Street, thinking about the night ahead and her boyfriend back home. She was an ocean and a continent away from Arthur and the lovely house they shared in Sausalito.

Her man was undoubtedly in the kitchen, chopping onions, checking the oven temperature. He was a chef with a growing online following, and was never more joyful than in his culinary lair. Serene enjoyed playing Robin to his Batman, though using a knife skillfully for cooking was not a gift God had given her.

Serene reached over to the heated towel rack, pulled off a fluffy white one, and wrapped it around her long, taut, brown frame. She could easily pass for a WNBA player (and sometimes did), though mixed martial arts were more her speed. She'd been approached for autographs and signed Lisa Leslie's name once or twice, hoping the basketball legend would never find out.

Serene moved into the bedroom, where Naughty by Nature's "Hip Hop Hooray" came out of a faux transistor radio on the bed's nightstand. The room had another musical anachronism as well: a mini Marshall amp by the bar.

Using her laptop, she surveyed a map of the area. She'd walked around earlier and gotten the lay of the land, but knowledge was king. London was very eccentrically laid out with crazy side streets, alleyways, and odd names. This wasn't a city neatly laid out on a grid, but a lovely hodgepodge where James Bond, Harry Potter, and Jack the Ripper easily coexisted in imagination and memory. It had only been a day but she already liked London. Now, to make it work for her.

Serene took the small elevator down, walked through the wood-paneled lounge area, handed her room key to the receptionist, and went out onto buzzing Dean Street. She made a left, walked past restaurants, hotels, and a private club before making another left onto Richmond Mews, a cul-de-sac that ended with a string of white lights and big windows as one entered the Soho Hotel.

As this neighborhood had once been the home of production companies, film distributors, and screening rooms, the Soho Hotel had become Hollywood's London location for junkets, touring musicians, and actors. Rising real estate prices had driven many media companies out of central London to Shoreditch, but many traveling musicians and actors still called the Soho Hotel their London home. As Serene entered the lounge, the actor Michael Sheen walked past her toward the elevators, while action stud Jason Statham knocked back a pint with two mates at the bar.

Serene glided pass Statham to a spot near the man she knew to be Alister McCord. He sat with a glass of top-shelf Scottish whiskey in a well-tailored blue suit, an eggshell-white shirt, and an exquisite haircut. He smelled like an ocean breeze and his eyes were a piercing blue.

Those blue eyes quickly surveyed Serene, studiously judging her shoulders, legs, and thighs. Serene would have been flattered if she hadn't known that underneath his stylish veneer was a corrupt exploiter of women. He slid Serene his business card, which said he was an *investment adviser*. But she knew that sex trafficking was what McCord was really invested in, and that he had deep connections to Russian mobsters that paid for his bespoke suits. Any legit business McCord did was funded on the backs of women imprisoned throughout Europe.

McCord thought Serene a prostitute. She upped the ante by replying that she was a dominatrix. Intrigued, McCord asked what roles she played.

"I can be a nurse or a nanny," she responded with her best Jamaican accent, "but spandex and paddles are what I do best. Do you enjoy being spanked?"

"What well-educated sire of the British isles doesn't, my dear?"

"I have a place a few blocks from here," she told him.

"Of course you do," he said. "I would expect nothing less. I have some time. Think you can accommodate me for forty minutes?"

"It will be your pleasure."

They exited out the bar's doors onto bustling Wardour Street. Drinkers clustered outside bars. Londoners sought out favorite restaurants or headed to the nearby theater district. Cars navigated Soho's tight streets as if the pedestrians were invisible. Soho had once been a tawdry home base for legendary gangsters and brothels. Despite the ongoing twenty-first-century upgrades, echoes of its sleazy past could still be heard.

One particularly dark sound emanated from Tyler's Court, an alley a few blocks from the hotel which once housed a brothel. Midway down the alley, the door was still there and Serene had the keys. McCord followed her up a stairway.

On the third landing, they entered a room with just a wooden table, chairs, leather belts, and a bottle of water.

"Bare bones, isn't it?" McCord observed just before Serene punched him in the stomach. When he bent over she caught his face with a knee. As he wobbled backward, Serene spun around and cracked a rib with a sidekick. McCord moaned and grabbed his right side. Serene tied his hands with leather straps and dragged him over to a chair.

Now fully aware of his predicament, McCord's veneer of proper English upbringing disappeared. He looked at Serene with the disgust of a man who truly hated women.

"You just want to be a man," McCord shouted, "but you have the wrong fuckin' equipment, cunt!"

Serene walked over to him and smiled. "I may have been born with the wrong equipment, but that doesn't mean I can't buy it, mate."

Back on Tyler's Court, Serene made a left onto Berwick Street and then another left onto narrow Walker's Court, which had once been filled with sex shops, strip clubs, and dirty deeds done dirt cheap. Like much of contemporary Soho, Walker's Court was modernized, cleaned up, sanitized. Still, a lively bit of the old grime could be found at a sex shop with pink windows.

When Serene walked up and made her request, the Englishman behind the counter leered from ear to ear. But Serene wasn't deterred or one bit self-conscious. She perused his offerings and, to the Englishman's satisfaction, purchased the biggest model. Now a satisfied customer, Serene strolled back down Berwick and onto Tyler's Court with a small grin.

When Serene entered, McCord stopped struggling with his bonds and stared at her. "What's in the bag, cunt?"

Serene said politely, "Something you are probably very familiar with." She pulled a long black dildo and bottle of lube from the bag, placing them on the table.

"I don't need the dildo," McCord with a snarl. "But I am certain your cunt needs the lube."

Serene didn't respond. She walked behind the handcuffed man with the dildo in one hand and the lube in the other. The suddenly flustered McCord shouted, "Get out from behind me, cunt!" With her foot, Serene tipped his chair forward and the trafficker fell, face-first, to the wooden floor.

Blood oozed from McCord's forehead and mouth. Serene pulled down his pants and underwear. McCord's voice, which had a lot of bass in it, reached a higher pitch now, like a soul singer going falsetto, as Serene squirted lube along the crack of his white ass. When she turned the vibrating dildo on, it sounded like the buzz of small propeller plane.

"Cunt, you wouldn't!"

"Oh, I would and I am," she said. "I need some names, though."

"What names?"

"What names and addresses you do think, pimp? Locations, safe houses, business partners. I'm not the police. There will be no due process. You help me, you maintain your dignity. If not, you become my bitch."

Alister McCord gave up names and locations in Paris, Morocco, and the UK, but wasn't very forthcoming about any connections in the US. Serene recorded him on her smartphone and whenever McCord's enthusiasm tailed off, she would bring that dildo up to his ear and let him feel the buzz.

This was a fruitful twenty minutes for Serene, well worth the flight over.

She told him, "I hope this isn't just a list of imaginary friends."

McCord lay awkwardly on the floor, tied up with his butt in the air. He wasn't a gangster really, so breaking him wasn't that hard. But he was a hateful pimp, which made Serene consider violating him anyway.

She forwarded the names to her connect Mildred Barnes in the US and waited to hear back. She chuckled looking at McCord, his bare ass paler than a December moon, his haughty demeanor a memory. She contemplated her next move. All she was responsible for was getting him here. His "disposal" was up to someone else, though she had been assured that he would not be murdered since she'd be the last person seen with him and London had more cameras per square foot than almost any city on the planet.

Her phone buzzed. The word *Go* appeared on her screen and she headed for the door.

"Where are you going, cunt?!"

Serene walked back over, turned on the vibrating dildo, and placed it next to his face. "It has been pleasant meeting you, Alister," she said. "Someone will be along shortly. I don't know what will happen to you, but hopefully it will be even more unpleasant than this."

Amid McCord's curses, Serene left the room, headed downstairs, and locked the door. In the noise of Soho on a Friday night, no one heard McCord scream.

Her night was done. Back to the bathtub. Tomorrow night, she was to encounter another prissy pimp. Apparently London was full of them.

CHAPTER FOUR
MADE IN AMERICA

Fuck Trump. Fuck Paul Ryan. Fuck chicken-neck McConnell and fascists disguised as Christians and scandal mongers masquerading as journalists and all the people who said there was no difference between Trump and Clinton.

D was watching CNN or MSNBC or something like that with the sound off, using the graphics projected under the talking heads to get a sense of what inhumanity was passing as government policy in the first year of the reign of Putin from Queens. Trump's election had been the triumph of the white rage that had been building during Obama's eight years, and this current brand of white supremacy was baked into the nation's DNA a lot like lynching and pious hypocrisy.

The image of Trump and his designated Uncle Tom, Dr. Ben Carson, appeared on the screen. D flashed back to the nineties when Trump's black friends were way cooler. D had worked security at upscale events where New York's new money congregated, at a time when Trump and hip hop were scandalous new forces on the social scene. D remembered #45 at Puff's white parties in the Hamptons, talking to Penny Marshall and eyeing Naomi Campbell. He remembered #45 at Moomba on Seventh Avenue gossiping about the boxing biz over a Dom P with Mike Tyson. He remembered Russell Simmons and Andre Harrell greeting Trump one night at Indochine before they all headed to a Fashion Week party.

What Trump shared with the hip hop moguls was that they were all outerborough kids obsessed with Manhattan props. Trump wanted mad fame so much he splashed his name on every surface he owned, like a graffiti tagger using gold block letters. His visionary branding had impacted hip hop. He preached, "Put your name on everything." His hip hop acolytes followed suit.

The exchange between Trump and hip hop wasn't a one-way street. When D watched the GOP debates he recognized a man working by the rules of a rap battle. He tagged his opponents with disrespectful nicknames ("Mr. Low Energy") and constantly sang his own praises with the superhuman certainty of a cocky MC. His GOP opponents thought they were there to talk policy. #45 was there to dis. Trump was his own bellowing hype man. He took out GOP contenders like Rakim did those seven MCs.

Obama was the first black president. Trump was the first rap-battle president. #45 promoted the culture's worst values (clueless capitalism, blatant misogyny, baseless boasting). So while D had despised conservatives before (Cheney, Rumsfeld, etc.) and doubted many liberals (de Blasio, Sanders, etc.), he thought Trump deserved a special place in hell for combining rap aesthetics with racism.

Whenever D's blood pressure rose and he grew fearful of the future, he remembered what his late mentor Dwayne Robinson used to say: "No one and nothing stays hot forever. This world is composed of cycles and epochs. Movements spawned by one generation are either evolved by the next one or totally rejected. Today's hero is tomorrow's jerk, and vice versa." Now Dwayne had been a music and cultural critic; politics had not been his specialty. But D thought his words were applicable to the dance of progressive and conservative, open-mindedness and dogma, that America was engaged in. Right now, the music of politics was ugly and simpleminded, like the melody in an idiot's head.

D switched off the cable-news mind maze, moved over to his laptop, and clicked on Spotify's Rap Caviar, a weekly selection of the newest jams from the white-hot center of twenty-first-century hip hop, like listening to Funk Flex at his Hot 97 peak. D knew he was moving into a maze of a different kind. Rap Caviar made hits and pushed the conversation forward. There were traces of the hip hop D had grown up with in Kendrick Lamar and Chance the Rapper, but most of the acts were trap-based, including Lil Daye, whose new "Hy Life" was number one on the Rap Caviar playlist.

D thought Dwayne Robinson would have loved this moment, a time similar to when band-based funk gave way to computers and drum machines, to when gospel became soul, to when singing yielded to rapping as the apex of black expression. And here D was, in the middle of it as a manager.

The irony was that his relationship with Lil Daye had developed because of R&B. D had only gotten into talent management because his friend Night and his longtime road manager Al Brown had begged him to join their team and help save Night's singing career. Al and D had squeezed a Grammy Award–winning album out of Night and gotten him back on the road after a self-imposed decade-long absence.

However, what finally got Night back on track were the contacts D had developed within the Koreatown business community to get the singer gigs creating nineties-style R&B tracks for K-pop bands. While the market in America was being deluged with MCs "singing" via auto-tune, Koreans still wanted real singers and heard the older melodies and production sounds with fresh ears. For the last year, Night had been shuttling between LA and Seoul on a monthly basis and had even cut a track with PSY, Mr. "Gangnam Style."

D's powers of resurrection had been even more impressive with the once-reclusive Dr. Funk. Dr. Funk had once been a giant star, but since the mideighties he'd become a soul diminished by drugs and mental illness. D had been very successful in mining the man's impressive catalog. He'd licensed classic songs, remake rights, and a couple of newer compositions to two Netflix shows, a Hulu special, and a national campaign for butter. Equally lucrative were special hologram shows for major corporations he'd developed with R'Kaydia. A hologram of Dr. Funk and his band, the Love Patrol, had gone on tour, performing songs from the classic *Chaos: Phase I* LP.

The highlight of these shows was when the real seventysomething Dr. Funk came onstage and did a duet with the eighties hologram of himself. It always brought down the house and got high six-figure paydays from Hewlett-Packard, Walmart, and Staples. (On the DL, a quarter of any new income Dr. Funk generated went to a fund to benefit victims of sexual violence, via a deal D had negotiated with one-time foe turned friend Serene Powers.)

After moving to LA, D had gone a bit Hollywood. He sold his life rights to a production company for a project called *The Accidental Hunter*, which centered around the time he'd saved white teen idol Bridgette Hayes from getting kidnapped by a motorcycle gang. There had also been a short-lived, awkward romance between the bodyguard and the singer that helped stoke interest in the project. Would it be a feature film or a miniseries? Could it be a franchise? Maybe make it a musical like *The Greatest Showman*? Maybe a procedural like *S.W.A.T.* with a different celebrity protected each week? Think of the cameos!

There were a dizzying, disorienting number of meetings in the film and TV game. D had gotten used to spitballin' meet-ups that resulted in nothing but spit. Maybe because the production company felt guilty, they'd made D a consulting producer on a comedy about a road man-ager, his first television credit.

The one thing he did absolutely like about film and TV people is that they got up early and spent most of their weekends reading. After years of late nights and afternoon wake-up calls, D was cool with a world where people actually showed up for breakfast meetings, where reading was a tool, not a luxury. Middle age was imminent and there was nothing more mortifying than being the old head in the cypher.

Yet here he was in Atlanta, listening to bits and pieces of various current hits, trying to suss out the competition and, on a personal level, refine his sense of what was and wasn't "lit." One night at a South Beach nightclub, the Brooklyn MC Asya Roc, an old client of D's, had shared a banquet with Lil Daye. Apparently, a big topic of conversation with millennial MCs was who among the older generation could be trusted in business. Aysa Roc told Lil Daye the true story of how D had prevented him from getting jacked at an underground boxing club and how the bodyguard had even inspired several records with stories from his days growing up in buck-wild Brownsville.

When Lil Daye sought a rep in LA, he wanted someone who was connected to film as well as music; an African American who under-stood the streets. D fit the bill perfectly. Now he was furiously playing catch-up on trap. Lil Daye didn't need D to manage the details of his recording career (the young man was very self-sufficient in that area) but he needed a trustworthy guide to the suit-and-tie folks.

D was still listening to Rap Caviar when a familiar number popped up on his smartphone.

"Yo D," Night said, "how's ATL treating you?"

"I'm good. Enjoying the hospitality, but I do miss LA, NY, and every other big city."

"ATL not cosmopolitan enough for you?"

"It's got its charms," D said, "but I've never loved landlocked cities."

"Nigga, you can't even swim."

They both cracked up at this.

"That doesn't mean I don't like looking at water."

Again they laughed, chuckling like old men on a park bench.

"Where are you at?" D asked. "Back from Seoul?"

"I'm good over there for now," Night said. "Did the tracks with Brown Eyed Girls and now I'm back in LA working on my stuff with some talented kids. Young dudes, but they can really play. Got some church in them too. I also got Thundercat on a track and I may sing on his next joint."

"Remember," D said, "I'm the one who turned you on to the scene out there in LA. Don't act like you just discovered the players in Cali."

"Which is why I wanna play you some of what I'm working on."

This excited D. "My e-mail is ready and waiting."

"No, my man," Night said. "This is music that needs to be heard face to ear. It's analog music. Shouldn't be compressed. It's got big nuts. Needs some room."

"You sounding cocky, Night. I like it."

"I'm not gassing you, D. It's good."

"You wanna come down here to Atlanta? I can fly you down. Won't even charge it against the money your ass owes me."

"Fuck you," Night said. "Sounding like a damn manager now. When you come back to LA, I'll play what I've been working on and you will be impressed."

"Word?"

"Word up, old school."

CHAPTER FIVE

NO CHURCH IN THE WILD

Ice bought two burners at Lenox Square and then picked up his order of faux chicken, peas and rice, and fried bananas from the nearby vegan spot. Armed with the electronics and sustenance he desired, the former hit man went up to his apartment, put his feet up on the glass coffee table, and turned on *SportsCenter*, keeping the sound off. The old-school clock on his wall read 6:25 p.m. so he had a few minutes to chow down before his weekly ritual.

Ice had gone vegan a year ago when his stomach started aching and a cute young woman in his acting class suggested he change his diet. The relationship hadn't gone far—he was both too old and too mysterious for her—but Ice was a star in class. There were layers of unspoken pain in him and even a gift for comedy. He suspected that trauma and humor were two sides of a coin. He'd inflicted enough pain to understand that people under pressure had an unending capacity for the ridiculous.

His acting classes had served a very practical role in his undercover life. It would never be enough to add hair, glasses, and weight. To truly disappear, Ice felt he had to change how he moved. That gangsta walk had been useful in Brownsville, East New York, and the other BK hoods he'd once stalked. Under the Southern sun, he needed to relax his body and warm up that physical armor so that he moved like a nine-to-five retiree. In the acting classes he dove into the role-playing exercises, moving as a cat, a dog, or any other animal that helped him erase his swagger and replace it with something that made his steps as anonymous as a broke-down bus driver. He'd always thought nine-to-five folks walked like kicked dogs. Now he embraced that puppy wobble, hoping to move like a middle-aged man at a multiplex matinee.

At 6:30 p.m. Ice texted a 917 area code with the words *Can you talk?* After a few moments the reply was *Yes.* Ice called.

A woman in her thirties answered and asked, "How are you, Big Poppa?"

"I'm okay N'Dya. Some drama though."

"Old or new?"

"Old. That's the only kind I have these days," Ice said with resignation. "How is Tiana?"

"Had a cold today so we kept her out of school."

"She there?"

"Doing homework. I don't wanna pull her away."

"I understand," he said, but any time talking with his granddaughter felt like a blessing. Trying to hide his disappointment he asked, "You need anything?"

"All the time," N'Dya said, and they both laughed. "What about you?"

"Can you check in on Kima?"

"Why you wanna know about that bitch all of a sudden?"

This was an old beef between the two women and Ice hated to bring Kima up, but he needed some eyes on his ex.

"Please," he said, "just check in on her. Need to know if she has any old drama too. Feel me?"

"Whatever," his daughter said with a sigh. "You know what I think about her triflin' ass."

Ice glanced at his clock: 6:47 p.m. "Gotta go. Me and you, N'Dya."

"Love you, Big Poppa."

Ice texted a 718 area code, writing, *Can we talk?* He watched LeBron James bulldoze a couple of Nets on his way to the hoop while he awaited a reply. That there were now NBA games in Brooklyn just subway stops from his old hood was a source of irritation. It was an injustice that he had to sit with the Atlanta Hawks' sorry-ass fans to watch ball when he and his old crew should have been courtside at the Barclays Center.

The second burner buzzed and the text read, *Get at me.* The phone rang five times before it was answered.

"Nigga, what's your goddamn problem? You knew it was me."

"I'm sorry," Pablo said, "I was just in the bathroom."

"I didn't call about your bowel movements. Keep that info to yourself. Now whatcha know?"

"There's a dude named C Dawg," Pablo said, his Puerto Rican accent a balm to Ice's ears, though what the man said was damned irritating. "Could be with the feds. He's back in East New York. He says he just got home. Based on his questions and what he knows and what business he's doing, I got my eye on him."

"Any of our people know his pedigree?"

"Another questionable nigga from Brevoort by the name of Fade says he does. Now, Fade says this C Dawg was related to Tracy."

"If my name comes out of this nigga's mouth, you need to handle him."

"Fade or C Dawg?"

"Shit, both if need be, but Fade 'cause he connects Tracy to us."

"I'm following up," said Pablo.

"How's business?"

"We got everything in order. Some real estate developers have been asking about that building you got on Pennsylvania Avenue. White folks trying to come over here, bro. You can check with me on Friday. Same time."

"Nigga, I'll reach out just like I always do. Don't set no dates or deadlines for me."

"I'm just saying it could be real money."

"Be ready with details next week." Ice hung up, stomped the two burners with his feet, and tossed the pieces in the garbage.

CHAPTER SIX

CARRIED AWAY

The delivery van was white and dingy with no distinctive markings. It was clearly being badly used by the villains leasing it. Serene had been trailing it as it wound its way through moneyed Knightsbridge on a journey out to Dalston. There was a tracking device on the van so she didn't need to be very close, but she wanted to be there when it stopped so that smooth motherfucker behind the wheel could feel her fist. She'd tracked Serge Schockweilder since he'd left the Chiltern Firehouse, a posh spot full of bold-faced names. But now Schockweilder was on a seedier mission and Serene was tracking his ass in a Mercedes.

The van was stopped at a red light when the back door popped open and a woman stumbled out in a thin, shiny, blue dress with matching shoes. She was light brown, beautiful, and obviously scared. She turned her head like a trapped animal unsure of which way to go. Schockweilder stormed out of the driver's-side door shouting, "Get back in the van!" From her car Serene saw another white man inside the van whose pants were down, shirt was off, body beet red.

The girl ran unsteadily toward an alley with Schockweilder coming after her. She fell after just a few steps and he grabbed her by her shoulder. "You little fucking cunt!" he yelled, jerking her to her feet, before he suddenly let go. The girl looked up and saw a blur of feet and hands cave in his stomach and bloody his right ear. She heard a cracking sound when a foot impacted his nose. His tailored suit was suddenly covered in blood. He tumbled to the ground. Then a woman's hand reached down to her and said softly, "Let's go, baby."

CHAPTER SEVEN

LIFE'S A BITCH

D liked Atlanta but really wanted to love it. In fact, he felt damn near disloyal for not fully embracing the ATL. It was where Dr. King had learned lessons that would help him reshape America. Generations of the black middle-class had been nurtured at Morehouse, Spelman, and the other HBCUs of the city. Despite being smack dab in the redneck state of Georgia, Atlanta had blossomed as a mecca where black elected officials ruled and black entrepreneurs could thrive. The best thirty minutes on television were named after the city and its stories reflected the centrality of Atlanta to African American identity.

And yet, for D, this sprawling metropolis never inspired deep love. It was a landlocked city and D found it quietly disturbing to gaze out his forty-third-floor hotel window and know there was no shore nearby, not even a river or a lake. More profoundly, Atlanta was a city that worked to mask the fact that it was nestled in the Deep South. It had remade itself into an international city, developing businesses as well as cultural and social institutions that befit a global destination. There were quality restaurants and museums. CNN was founded there, beaming news and nonsense across the world 24/7/365. A healthy percentage of all the visual content on screens in the US (and the world) was shot there, much of it in a studio owned by a black man named Tyler Perry. No doubt it was truly Hollywood South.

Still, its very Southernness rankled D. Every place in the US had a legacy of racism. His beloved Brooklyn was no exception. Yet there was something about being in the place where white folks had happily enslaved Africans that, on some subconscious level, made him uneasy. Moreover, the economic and social restrictions that were instituted after the Civil War still shackled black folks, something that was clear when you traveled into Georgia away from Atlanta's cocoon. For him, that heavy legacy was not obscured by the way Southern whites would say *Yes sir* or *No ma'am* to black folks they encountered. Times had changed, but there was so much blood in the soil.

From a pure business point of view, it made sense to get a place in Atlanta and put down some roots. Aside from the Lil Daye relationship, there were myriad investment and real estate opportunities, especially if he brought his NY/LA income with him. Coastal cash went far in Atlanta. The city was definitely a hottie, but so far, D's courtship hadn't gotten past hand-holding. The fact that his favorite living father figure called Atlanta home was a major plus. Even when the old man went on one of his riffs in the hotel dining room, D couldn't hide his affection.

"It used to be easier to be a man. The rules of engagement were clearer. You made a living, provided for your loved ones, and learned to handle trouble. You drank on the weekends. Gambled either money or limbs for recreation. Women wanted you to make them feel safe, especially if they grew up in the ghetto, and they wanted you to be forceful with them. It helped to be cool. It was good to be able to tell jokes or know a good one when you heard it. You didn't go spouting off about your feelings. You kept your own counsel. You didn't rat on friends— unless they went too damn far. You didn't cry in front of people. You did what had to be done 'cause it was your place to do it and no one would do it for you. Your home was your castle. You prayed to God.

"You sang the blues. You shined your shoes till they glowed like brass. You took pride in your work—no matter how bullshit the pay. You kept your word. Your word was everything so you didn't give it easily. You loved your country as much as it loved you. You loved your people as long as they loved themselves. You pissed standing up. You fucked any old way that it worked out. When the good Lord came to take you home, you thanked Him for paying attention. End of goddamn story."

D thought about debating Fly Ty, shooting holes in the assumptions, evasions, and outright lies embedded in his old friend's monologue. But that would have just wasted their precious time together.

The retired New York City detective was now as skinny and brown as an old roadside telephone pole. His eyes were milky and yellow, his brows the rusty gray of poured concrete, his cheekbones sharp as elbows under a basket. His mustache was thin like the heels on a woman's high-priced shoe. He wore a brown pinstripe suit, loafers, a beige tie with a stickpin, and a straw hat. Every now and then, Fly Ty Williams unleashed a deep cough that made the table rattle, which they both acknowledged wordlessly but didn't comment on. No point now.

Back in the crack-saturated Brownsville of the midnineties, Fly Ty Williams had been a surrogate father to forlorn young D, especially after D's real father departed for parts unknown. So it was always good to see Fly Ty, even if his steady physical deterioration was like a knife to D's gut. Fly Ty was dying. Prostate cancer was doing its nasty work. Chemo was an option but Fly Ty's thought was, *For what?*

"I'm already bald and skinny," Fly Ty said. "Lose any more weight and I'ma just disappear."

"We can't have you disappearing, Fly Ty," D said. "Not until you give me the name of your tailor."

"Shit, I'm keeping that fool in business. Every time I lose a few pounds I got to get everything tightened. I can't have my clothes hang off my ass like one of these 'Bama-ass bangers down here."

"I thought you liked being in style," D teased.

"Style? Yeah. Twentieth-century style is fine with me," Fly Ty said. "Can't fuck with what passes for cool these days. People can't coordinate worth a shit. It's like they think clothes are a flashing light. I need my shades on just to walk through the mall without going blind."

Fly Ty spent most afternoons walking up and down Lenox Square. His concession to missing New York was to watch the shoppers and look through windows, occasionally posting up in the food court to Google big-legged Southern ladies and imagine what pickup lines he would have used a couple of decades earlier.

"So D," he said, "I can tell by your disposition and body language that shit is deep. Let's get to it."

D related what he'd been told by Ice without saying where the info came from. To admit Ice and he were in contact would be revealing more than D was prepared to, knowing Fly Ty would be upset by his connection to the notorious hit man.

Fly Ty listened quietly and then said, "Agent Conrad, huh? I believe I know him. If he's the same guy, we worked together on a case involving human trafficking and kidnapping in the basement of a housing project. Baby pimps paid off the janitor for access to some rooms by the boiler. Those folks had the place decked out with red lights, multiple beds, and dividers like those Korean spas. Some girls did it for money, but once they got locked in that basement they were rarely allowed to leave.

"The cousin of one of the girls heard she was down there and got word to me. I got the feds involved because word was they were moving these girls across state lines to Jersey and even Connecticut. We busted in and they had four girls down there. All four underage. These baby pimps were trading girls with a network of other folks around the city and the region. Dark-web stuff. Some of their 'partners' had Asian and Caribbean girls. You could order to your taste.

"You'd be surprised at how many of these girls ended up in Williamsburg. Those bearded motherfuckers over there had no problem messing with black and brown poontang."

"Poontang? You are seventy, aren't you?"

"I may be old but I don't have no FBI agents calling around about me."

"Point taken. So what about this Conrad? Do you feel you know him well enough to give him a call?" D asked.

"No, I don't. But maybe someone else I worked with can. Need to find the right guy to call him with the right excuse. It's interesting about this guy—is he doing this as part of a real FBI investigation into Eric Mayer's death or was he just a close friend? It's a missing-person case that just became a homicide. But they must know this cat was corrupt, and digging into it would expose corruption at the Bureau . . . Okay, now that we know you are in danger of being connected to a dead rogue FBI agent, how's your personal life?"

"Well, that's a crazy shift in topic."

"I don't have any kids and you don't have any kids. That means I don't have any chance of having a grandson or granddaughter, and I ain't happy about it."

"Fly Ty, you know my situation," D said.

"People with the virus been having kids left and right," Fly Ty said. "In fact, with all the pills and treatments out there, there's only a very small chance a child would be born with it. So that ain't an excuse."

"You've been surfing the web."

"What else I got to do?" Fly Ty said sourly. "Listen, you need to wash your feet, change your socks, and toss your old sneakers."

"What the hell are you talking about?"

"I'm saying you gotta start all over like you have never walked before. You can laugh all you want but this is a time to link up with a woman and procreate. I read what's going on."

"You have a woman?"

"Course I do," Fly Ty said. "It's nature's way. I keep company with one of the ladies at the retirement village. Caroline is from Memphis. Nice Southern gal. I ain't twenty and she ain't twenty. I ain't saying nothing goes on, but I am good without all the drama. But *you* need a good woman 'cause it's like athlete's foot out here: you walk around naked too long and you bound to catch something."

D just nodded. *When you right, you right.*

CHAPTER EIGHT
FORMATION

Back at the hotel, Serene ran the bath for Anika Selam and gave the slender young women one of the hotel's comfy white bathrobes. There were bruises on her wrists and ankles and a couple on her back. Anika shook when Serene touched her, as if she expected to be slapped. Serene gently guided Anika into the big tub's soapy water. For a moment, Serene thought the young woman might drown since she seemed so uncertain of herself. When she ducked her head under the water, Serene pulled her right back up, which made Anika giggle. She just wanted to blow bubbles. Suddenly, they were sharing a laugh. Despite all Serene had imagined her going through, the young woman's smile was dazzling white. Serene went into the bedroom and called Mildred Barnes, who was not happy about Serene's decision-making.

"That's not why I sent you over there," Barnes scolded from across the Atlantic. She usually had a very neutral Midwestern accent, but there was spice in her voice tonight, which amused Serene. "We need you to help shut down *networks*, not save one girl at a time. That's for NGOs."

"I was not gonna leave her out in the street," Serene said firmly. "She figured out a way to get out of that van. She wasn't helpless—she just needed assistance. She wants to go home. We should make that happen."

Well aware that once Serene had made a decision, it was damn near impossible to change her mind, Barnes said, "All right. Okay. Let me make some calls."

Serene stuck her head back in the bathroom and watched Anika pour shampoo on her head and slowly begin washing her hair. Stretched out in the large tub, her brown skin surrounded by white bubbles, it was the first time Anika hadn't been extremely stressed out since she'd been kidnapped by the traffickers in Rome. She breathed deeply, looking up at the ceiling, and realized that this was the life she'd imagined for herself. That was before the reality of Europe had handcuffed her body and brutalized her soul. Serene saw tears come down Anika's face and just closed the door, knowing she had no words to soothe her.

Fifteen minutes later, Barnes called. "In about ninety minutes a woman will ring you. Make sure the girl is ready. Here's the thing: I had to loan you out."

"Loan me out?"

"These people and I have collaborated before. They have different goals than we—or I—have. But I think you'll get along."

"I promised Arthur I'd be back home in two days."

"I understand that," Barnes said. "But it was your decision to pick up that girl, so this is on you."

"Okay," Serene said. "What do they want me to do?"

"In exchange for them arranging to get this girl back to Africa, you will have to pick up an object for them."

"Something stolen?"

"Stolen, yes," Barnes admitted. "But not what you think."

"I don't like this."

"Fine," Barnes said. "If you trust the UK authorities to do the right thing by this girl, then I can call it off."

Barnes knew she'd spoken the magic words. Serene's cynicism about government kicked in and she agreed to the plan.

Serene dug out a T-shirt that kind of fit Anika and some jeans that, after they cut an extra hole in her belt, looped around the young woman's slender hips. Serene wanted to burn her dress but figured it might contain her captor's DNA, so she slid it into a hotel laundry bag. They were watching season one of *Empire* on Serene's laptop when the hotel phone rang. "We're downstairs. Please join us." The woman's accent was strange and musical.

They were met in the lobby by a tiny light-brown woman with a thick blackbird cage of hair, large shining eyes, and a worried smile. She said her name was Helen, but Serene didn't believe that for second. There was a black Benz outside to transport Anika.

"Where are you taking her?"

Helen said, "To somewhere she'll blend in until we can arrange transport for her. Better if I don't tell you more."

Behind the wheel of the Benz was a dark-chocolate, round-faced woman named Soa. Anika didn't want to get in the car until Soa spoke a few words of Hausa to her. Anika nodded her head in recognition, then turned and gave Serene a big hug. Serene could feel the young woman's bones against her body. She watched Soa steer the car into the London night.

"Can I buy you a drink?" Helen said.

"I don't really drink," Serene said, "but I know we have to talk."

Helen gave an impish smile. "You Americans are so healthy. No worries. I'll drink for both of us."

The two found an empty sofa at the nearby Soho House, where Helen ordered a chardonnay and Serene had chamomile tea with honey. Serene had a million questions but started with her accent.

"I'm Ethiopian on my mother's side and German on my father's," Helen explained, clearly used to answering this question. "So you are hearing English spoken with hints of German and Amharic. Plus, I speak Spanish too, so that's in the mix."

"And how do you know Mildred Barnes?"

"I don't. But my friend William does. He called me from Paris. He runs our little operation. We don't do what you do, which is really great by the way, but we have another mission. You deal with *current* evil. We try to correct the evils of colonialism—in our own way."

"Okay," Serene said, "sounds good. But what is it you do?"

"Well, we aren't the Avengers or anything," Helen said slyly. "But when we do feel like superheroes, we joke that we're the Liberators."

"The Liberators? Okay, I may have that glass of wine."

"Oh, it's just a nickname," Helen said, smiling. "I don't have a cape in my bag or anything. Now I have tell you, very respectfully, that we'd like help collecting the three medallions of Ethiopia."

"Damn, that sounds like some Indiana Jones stuff."

"Except we aren't just some white men rummaging around Africa in khakis," Helen said. "We are Africans rediscovering ourselves."

"Okay," Serene said, "this is all very deep and a little hard to digest. But I know how crazy what I'm doing is, so I'm in no position to judge anybody. Please, tell me what you want me to do."

"Have you ever been to Berlin?"

Excerpt from *The Plot Against Hip Hop* by Dwayne Robinson (2011):

The dance between creativity and commerce for black artists in

America is always fraught since the very gifts that liberate the soul are easily commodified into simple formulas that diminish the spirit, transforming deep passion into disposable product. Hip hop has manifested in so many creators embracing a limited, essentialist menu of stories and emotions that narrowed the MC and their audience's humanity. To be a thug or a gangsta bitch or a backpack MC was to be a mythological persona crafted to be easily understood and marketed, fitting into expectations of black life in a nation for whom stereotypes are reality.

Why think about the complexity of any individual life when through the right clothes, slang, and graphics you can telegraph your message—no need to think. Just enjoy your synthetic black experience and kick back with a cold brew or a blunt. The black Supermen of hip hop are just as phony as Rambo or Luke Skywalker, but those folks are acknowledged to be "actors," while MCs (often as essential parts of their promotional efforts) cling to authenticity when, in fact, they are "acting" their asses off. It can be a lucrative ploy but it literally sells them (and their audiences) short.

In that respect, self-taught iconoclasts like KRS-One, Scarface, and Kanye West have invariably seemed more credible to me as artists than always-"on message" performers like 50 Cent or Snoop, who work specific versions of themselves like Halloween masks. To be human is to err and make situational decisions not driven by a focused philosophy, but the swinging pendulum of life. Consistency is for salesmen, brand managers, and politicians. The hip hop artist who can resist one-note messaging risks his or her commercial power but, in exchange, can represent the multiplicity of true black identity in all its messy beauty. Sadly, few heed that call.

CHAPTER NINE
DNA.

D was on the treadmill at the Sunset Boulevard Equinox watching CNN on one of the big screens hanging from the ceiling. Another black man shot by the police. But the headline of the day was Trump firing FBI director James Comey. More blood on the ground. More lawlessness in DC. Bright LA sun came in from the big windows. Women in formfitting multicolored workout leotards sashayed by with Kim Kardashian eyebrows. Men, a healthy percentage of them gay, lifted weights, monitored each other's reps, and talked of parties past and future. D was in the middle of this well-appointed workout facility, one of the few black male clients. A couple of buff brothers were trainers, helping their white clients achieve maximum Southern California perfection. D's body was on the treadmill but his mind was several million miles away.

Trayvon Martin in Florida. Eric Garner in New York City. Michael Brown in Ferguson, Missouri. Laquan McDonald in Chicago. Tamir Rice in Cleveland. Walter Scott in South Carolina. Alton Sterling in Baton Rouge. Philando Castile in Minnesota.

Those were just the twenty-first-century names that popped into his head, but you could go back to Emmett Till in 1955 and then go back to the boys, men, girls, and women who'd been lynched, whose broken, charred, and disfigured bodies hung like tortured black leaves on Southern trees. All those white folks gathered, as if for a picnic or a town fair, to enjoy state-sanctioned murder. It was a legacy of authorized death that began with overseers in slavery days and that had never really stopped. It had just transformed with the times, part of our national language, like baseball and guns.

Though all black people were subject to this violence, there seemed to be a special role in this serialized drama for the destruction of black men, especially from adolescence to midforties. It wasn't a surprise that black gangs had always proliferated. The protections for black male life were so suspect that any form of community, no matter how self-destructive, was attractive in a world where your every affirmative gesture made you suspect.

Twice in his life D had felt especially vulnerable to law enforcement whims, each encounter as arbitrary as a nightmare. On the Upper East Side, D had been walking toward Lexington Avenue when a van full of police pulled up next to him. Suddenly, D was surrounded. He stopped dead in his tracks awaiting an explanation. None was offered. Instead, an older cop turned to a younger one. "Is this him?" the older cop asked. The younger cop looked D over, said, "No," and then the police scampered back into the van without an apology.

D had been in a long-distance relationship with a makeup woman working at the Black Entertainment Television studio when it was still in DC. Cheryl was a pear-shaped beauty with big eyes and golden-brown skin who studied the Yoruba religion when she wasn't putting eyeliner and pancake on R&B singers. Cheryl had taken a liking to the big man dressed in black and given him her business card, saying he could use a bit of powder on his bald dome. D had happily taken the bait and began chatting with her on the phone, which quickly escalated to Amtrak weekend rendezvous in NYC and DC.

On one particular afternoon, he'd come down to DC to hit a museum and have dinner, but once he'd entered her apartment, a kiss became a nibble, and then a full meal on her mud-cloth bedspread. D hadn't told her he was HIV positive yet and, despite her reassurance that it was okay, he'd worn a condom. Cheryl and D had tremendous chemistry and he'd wondered afterward whether they had a future.

It was fall and D had worn a black leather jacket that he was zipping up when they stepped outside her apartment building. Three DC police cruisers screeched up to the curb. Cops rushed out with guns drawn. Cheryl screamed. A white cop pointed an automatic at D's face. He took a deep breath. He could see right down the barrel. D put up his hands, which were then pulled behind his back and cuffed. It was a multiracial bunch of police but the man in charge was white and had officer's bars.

He had been stuffed into the back of a cruiser. He could hear Cheryl yelling at the police, but D stayed calm. Next to him was another black man, about his age, wearing a shiny brown leather jacket. The car pulled off and D craned his neck to see Cheryl being restrained by an officer. Between the policemen in the front seat and the guy next to him, D figured out that there had been a robbery by "a black man in a dark leather jacket" and that they were headed for a lineup.

D, who'd seen so many family, friends, and clients in similar situations, worked to suppress his anxiety at being one trigger finger away from death. He told himself he hadn't been shot and that he hadn't robbed anyone and he had a witness who could give the cops intimate details of his actions of the last few hours that would make the station house envious. D had even smiled, trying to focus on that truth and not the reality that he was sitting on a hard seat in the back of a police car with his hands cuffed and the circulation to his fingers disappearing.

The cruiser stopped at a curb and D was pulled out and made to stand motionless with a policeman holding his arm. A black man, an employee or a customer, stuck his head out of the store, looked at D, and nodded—yes, he had robbed the store. Now D's cool front collapsed and he began speaking rapidly about how he'd been with Cheryl and how wrong that crazy motherfucker in the store was!

D was trying to think if he knew anyone in the security game in DC, someone on the force or even an attorney. A weekend in a DC jail was not what he had in mind when he'd arrived at Cheryl's place.

Thankfully, two more people came out of that store and both shook their heads. D was not the perpetrator. The handcuffs came off and D felt his butt cheeks unclench. The officer walked over to D and asked if he'd like a ride back to where they'd picked him up. There was no way he was getting back in that cruiser. "Good luck, bro," he said to the brother in the brown leather jacket and then headed back in the direction of Cheryl's place. He wasn't quite sure where he was going, but anyplace was better than where he had been.

Cheryl had tear-filled eyes when he finally got back to her apartment and they ordered in, watching movies on HBO and then making love again until their bellies glistened with sweat. D had planned on staying the entire weekend but after a couple of phone calls, he told Cheryl had to get back to the Apple. Though it wasn't a conscious decision, he didn't return to DC again for two years, passing on gigs that would have taken him to BET and passing on invitations to visit Cheryl. She came up to New York a few times, but something had changed for D, and the relationship ended with a long-distance phone call.

D remembered all this while watching the TV. He sighed deeply, pressing stop on the treadmill, and looked at a protest march on CNN for the slaying of a black man for holding a smartphone some cop claimed was a gun.

Through ambition, access, and a couple of accidents, D had survived the ghetto gauntlet. Some would say he was a winner. Truth was,
he was just one awful moment away from death every time a bigoted,
fearful, inexperienced police officer gazed his way. D looked down at his
watch. 8:15 LA time, 11:15 ATL time. He had a call in fifteen minutes.

Well, D wasn't dead yet. Things to do. Money to make. Dreams
to remember. Goals to fulfill. Food to eat. Women to love. Days to fill.
Night to night to night. Moments. So many moments. It could all end in
a second. Until then, D would not, could not, live in fear. He wiped the
sweat off his brow, smelled the musk from under his arm, and smiled.
He was alive and fuck you to them all—every last one.

CHAPTER TEN
NICE FOR WHAT

O nce again soaking in that big London hotel room bathtub, every muscle in Serene's upper back ached. It felt like her left rotator cuff had a slight tear and there were bruises on both shoulders. It wasn't deep pain, but she wasn't looking forward to the long trip back in coach across the Atlantic.

This discomfort was soothed by what she'd accomplished in London. Someone could argue that releasing one or two girls was a drop in the bucket compared to all the humans trafficked across the globe. But every girl rescued was a life saved, a family reconnected, and a little less evil on a planet. This wasn't the life she'd expected, but it felt like a righteous one, and the path of the righteous was never easy. She'd been a soldier. She'd been an athlete. She'd been a teacher. Now, she was all those things and more.

Serene Powers's odyssey had started one Monday morning at the Westlake Academy outside of San Francisco. While teaching the morning English lesson, she'd noticed that Alicia German wasn't in class. Alicia, a caramel teen with fashionably curly hair, was precocious, smart, and way too infatuated with her own Instagram selfies.

Previously, Serene had found Alicia crying in the girl's restroom. Her father Theo had a gambling problem and had stolen money Alicia had stashed in her room for a class trip to the San Francisco MOMA.

"Where's your mother?" Serene asked.

"Dead," Alicia said, "in a car accident."

The next time they spoke about it, Alicia said her mother had drowned swimming. Serene checked the school records and found that her mother had actually died of a gunshot wound. Her father Theo had initially been charged with manslaughter but the DA hadn't pressed charges.

After reading that, Serene kept an eye on Alicia, looking for bruises on her arms and legs. She'd dropped her off at home on a couple of occasions, met her father, and seen rage in his eyes. She was sure they'd tangle one day.

Alicia didn't show up for school for a second day. This time, Serene cornered her best friend Elise, a sly girl whose assurances that she didn't know why Alicia wasn't in class rang false. Serene took her concerns to the principal, a stoic man named Josh Adams, who politely told her that the head of school security would look into it. Serene was still relatively new to the school so she didn't want to be too aggressive with her boss.

In the teacher's room, Serene used her iPhone to search Instagram for Alicia's account, but she needed to be approved and she got cold feet. Instead, she searched Elise's public account and its many pictures of teenagers in skimpy outfits and heavy eye makeup. A photo taken over the weekend at the Paradise Club caught her eye. The Paradise was a local spot no underage girl should have been in. Tagged in the photo with Elise was Alicia, wearing too much makeup and few clothes, and a sketchy dude with arms around both their young necks. He was identified as *@DaMagnificent1*.

DaMagnificent1 was brown, lean, and had the smug handsome face of a certified asshole. His fingers, wrist, neck, and teeth were bedazzled in gold and diamonds, like he was 2 Chainz on a budget. His profile described himself as *party promoter, playa, and pussy trainer.*

DaMagnificent1's Instagram account was full of pics of young women of the barely legal persuasion at the Paradise Club and other local venues. Serene's stomach rumbled when she spotted a post of Alicia sitting behind the wheel of a Tesla with DaMagnificent1 in the passenger seat flashing a victor's smile. Rifling through the promoter's pictures, Serene noticed other faces from the school's hallways. Apparently, the door policy at the Paradise Club didn't include checking IDs.

These images drove Serene back to Adams's office. Considering that his students were involved, Serene expected some serious anxiety when she showed the principal the DaMagnificent1/Paradise photos.

"We're aware there's a problem with the Paradise Club," Adams said matter-of-factly. "We've had complaints from parents about that place and we've passed those concerns on to the police."

"Shouldn't we alert the police that we potentially have a missing student?"

Adams said, "I've already spoken to Mr. German today and he said Alicia's just been sick."

"Did you ask to speak to her?"

"I did and he said she was sleeping."

"I've had run-ins with him before," Serene said.

"Yes," Adams replied coldly, "which is why you need to let me and the sheriff's office handle this. I appreciate your concern. Thanks for alerting me, and if anything is seriously amiss, we'll find out."

Serene, who'd only been at the school about a year, realized that this was her cue to leave. Of course she'd let the authorities handle things. But Serene knew leaving government employees as the chief protectors of young women was always a questionable decision.

Unsure how to proceed, Serene decided to clear her head and went over to the gym after work. Not an Equinox or 24 Hour Fitness, but a gym where people practiced the fine art of violence. Serene had gotten interested in mixed martial arts in the service and found it therapeutic after intense verbal engagement with teenage girls.

Actually, saying she got "interested" is seriously understating Serene's involvement with MMA. She'd learned to scrap on the streets of Richmond, a tough Bay Area town that made Oakland seem like a resort. In the army she'd refined her wrestling skills, and not just in the gym. The dirty secret of women's enlistment in combat zones was how many rapes and, in Serene's case, attempted rapes occurred by latrines and in the field. When a soldier attacked her after a late-night bathroom break, she'd nearly had to blind him with two thumbs to the right eye. In the fallout, Serene saw firsthand how the words *rape*, *consent*, and *seduction* would all be commingled in official status reports.

Anita Gibson was waiting on her at the gym. Anita, a tough white blonde with a flaming-red bird tattoo across her back, was a skilled Muay Thai fighter, capable of knocking out opponents with an elbow or knee. Anita was on the MMA circuit and promoting protein drinks on Instagram, wearing outfits showcasing her impressive six-pack, for cash which she brought home her to her husband and two sons.

Still, she'd found it hard to get the best of Serene, who was adept at clinch fighting, a style that allowed her to neutralize Anita's skill advantage. Serene specialized in keeping opponents close so she could inflict pain with knee thrusts or flip them on their backs to pound their face and upper body. This ground-and-pound approach was frowned upon in women's MMA, one reason Serene didn't want to go pro. She was afraid sport fighting could become therapy, and in some crazy flashback, she'd really hurt someone.

No worries on this day. Anita easily dominated Serene in three two-minute bouts.

"So what's going on?" Anita asked afterward. "I never kick your ass—at least not this easily."

Serene forced a laugh and then talked about her concerns regarding Alicia, DaMagnificent1, and the Paradise Club.

"I've heard nothing but bad things about that place," Anita said. "My husband and I went there one time to dance. When I went to the restroom I saw some really young girls in there doing coke. Back at the bar, some guy had slipped Rich a card and told him to check out some website if he was looking for something *fresher* than what he'd come in with."

"Fucking bold," Serene said.

"I tore than card to shreds and we left. So who knows what happened to your student at that place."

"You think the cops know about what's going on there?"

"How could they not?" Anita said. "But knowing and doing something aren't the same thing."

Over the previous five years, three high school girls from the area had disappeared. Alicia would make it four. There were whispers of a serial killer in the region. The FBI had even sent a profiler to the city. It sounded convenient to Serene, like blaming it all on the boogeyman. The local police had a human-trafficking department of two people who'd done an underwhelming presentation at the school. Based on Serene's army experience, she was skeptical.

So, against the advice of Adams, Serene didn't head home, but over to the small wood-framed house Alicia German shared with her father. The place was in need of TLC just like the people inside. It took ten rings before the front door cracked open. Theo German stuck his head out and gazed dolefully at Serene. He had a potbelly, a scruffy beard, and the hostile demeanor of a man who hadn't been happy in years.

"You ever heard of minding your business?" Theo barked by way of greeting.

"I wanna see Alicia."

"I bet you do," he said. "I look at you and you know what I see?"

"I don't care what you see, Mr. German. I need to talk to your daughter."

Theo sneered. "I see a lesbo and I seen you wanna make a lesbo-in-training of my daughter. That's why you're here."

"Let me see Alicia!"

Theo slammed the door. The force of it shook the porch and made Serene take a step back. She began yelling Alicia's name, walking around the house and asking her student to respond. A couple of neighbors peeked out their windows but the blinds and windows of Theo German's house stayed closed. When two sheriff's deputies drove up, Serene put her hands up and tried to explain her actions. That's when Theo, in a dirty blue bathrobe, Adidas slip-ons, and a black do-rag, popped out of the house and said the magic words: "Officers, I wanna press charges."

Handcuffed and pissed, Serene soon found herself in the back of a patrol car. Her temper didn't cool at the station, where the focus of the detectives' questioning wasn't where was Alicia, but why a schoolteacher was screaming outside a student's house. Serene was already hot but went nearly nuclear when they wanted to know "the nature" of Serene's relationship with Alicia.

"Are you fucking crazy?" she said in a tone that clearly made a question mark optional.

Theo's statement had basically been: my daughter is a runaway and I believe it was because Serene has been aggressively pursuing her for a lesbian relationship. Rather than endure further harassment, his daughter had run away. Theo's evidence? Well, Serene Powers was an amateur MMA fighter and everyone knew those girls didn't like dick.

It got worse. One of the detectives, a very dry, pale man in his forties, looked at an Instagram photo of Alicia and said, "Well, she *is* cute."

Serene wanted to leap across the table and slam him to the ground. She, however, had enough restraint to know that her teaching career was already hanging by a slender thread. If this incident got back to Adams (and how could it not?), her job was in danger.

By the time Arthur Ellis arrived at the precinct, the police had charged her with disturbing the peace but had also agreed to look into Alicia's relationship with the promoter DaMagnificent1. When she walked into the station's waiting area, there was her boyfriend sitting hunched over in a chair, watching himself cook on YouTube. He was viewing diagnostics, concerned that his talk about healthy wines wasn't going to match the views of last week's episode on vegan beef.

"Hey, bae," he said, wrapping Serene in his long arms. His thick black beard caressed her forehead and fragrant spices tickled her nose.

Arthur had the fingers of an artist and the slim, firm build of a former gymnast. He was the only man Serene had ever known who felt like home to her.

In Arthur's car, Serene related her day, all the while marveling at his sweetness and good heart. Between the army and her MMA hobby, Serene had spent much of her life around violent, driven people for whom there was honor in combat, but who had a hard time with mundane moments. Arthur was as far from those people as you could get. He was passionate about vegan cuisine and spent most days working on recipes, prepping food, and studying YouTube analytics.

"Bae," he often said, "we'll buy our first home off my YouTube subs and our second when I have my vegan-restaurant empire up and running. I'm gonna make people healthy even if they resist, kicking and screaming. Gonna put pictures of Trump eating at McDonald's on my website. That should scare up a lot of business." Arthur had several million subscribers on YouTube, was working on a cookbook for a New York publisher, and had been approached by vegan establishments in SF and LA about joining their staff. It was just a matter of time before he broke big.

Because Arthur made his money digitally, he wasn't concerned that Serene's "well-intentioned tantrum" would affect his business. He was definitely concerned for Alicia ("Her father is absolutely involved in whatever happened to her"), but felt like things were at a dead end.

Serene, exhausted from her crazy day, agreed. The whole affair would have concluded right there for Serene had she not received an e-mail from Elroy Biggs, one of the more indolent students in her morning English class. Elroy was a lumpy, overgrown man-child with sad eyes who was skating through school on an athletic scholarship. He wasn't the type to send late-night e-mails about English class.

His message read: *Miss Powers, sorry to get at you at night. I know you have been looking for Alicia from English class. A friend went to the gray house on the corner of Elm and Broadhurst. It was a place where you could get girls. He saw Alicia there, he says. He knew her from the Paradise. She didn't know him. That's all he told me. Hope that helps.*

Serene figured Elroy's "friend" was, in fact, Elroy. Guess ho houses don't have an age limit, she thought. She contemplated going to Elroy's house and dragging him to the police precinct. But that would expose the kid to embarrassing questions. Or she could call the police herself and pass on the tip. Then a crazy idea got her out of bed. She walked past Arthur in the kitchen on the way to the garage.

"Bae," Arthur said, "shouldn't you be gettin' some rest?"

"Can't rest," she said. "Not yet."

Under a dusty green tarp in the corner was an army locker. Inside were bits and pieces of her warrior life. She pulled out several heavy items and brought them into the kitchen, placing a gun, night-vision goggles, and a small explosive device on the table.

Arthur set down his fork and pushed aside the faux chicken he was preparing. "You," he said, "are about to propose something crazy."

Two hours later, Serene was in handcuffs again. So were a motley crew of pimps and thugs, including an outraged DaMagnificent1. A heavily sedated Alicia was on her way to a local hospital. News crews broadcast in front of a once-cute gray home with its front door blown off. The phrases "vigilante," "explosive device," "human trafficking," and "teenage girls" took this event from small-town oddity to viral event.

One website labeled Serene Powers "a real-life Batwoman" and featured a Facebook picture of her in a MMA outfit. The next morning, she was suspended by principal Adams "pending review by the school board." Arthur's YouTube cooking channel was flooded with comments, both insulting and amused, that had nothing to do with his culinary experiments. It wasn't a great day to be Serene Powers.

Yet it was. It would be the day Serene's life changed. A woman named Mildred Barnes called, identifying herself as "a friend of stolen women." She invited Serene for tea the next day at one the area's most expensive restaurants.

Sitting at an outdoor table was a refined-looking middle-aged white woman wearing a white blouse that matched her bright white hair and contrasted nicely with her red jacket, skirt, and pumps. On her right lapel was a small American flag. To any student of history, she resembled the late Texas governor Ann Richards. To Serene, she looked like the chairwoman of a Republican fund-raising event.

When Serene approached, Mildred stood and greeted her with a small hand and a firm grip. "Such a pleasure to meet you, Serene," she said.

After they sat down Serene asked, "Okay, what is this about?"

Mildred said firmly, "It's about saving women."

"You work for some charity?"

The middle-aged woman smiled. "I founded my own little organization."

"Which is?"

"It has no name," Mildred said. "There is no public record. I fund it myself. I've been looking for someone like you, Serene. A woman with the skills and attitude to hold people accountable."

"What does that mean?"

"The rich preying on women, children, and the poor is nothing new. The British did it for centuries using their class structure—incestuous bloodlines and all—as an excuse. They suppressed their own poor, their Irish neighbors, and their colonial subjects. The British refined a system of oppression and transported it around the globe, along with all the European colonizing cousins.

"Now the weak and the young are at the mercy of all manner of villain. ISIS and al-Qaeda traffic to buy weapons and use slave labor till the workers drop dead. The Mafia, the Yakuza, MS-13, the Russian mob, and every gang of greedy fucked-up men everywhere, including Wall Street. But it is the lust, greed, and basic depravity of the penis-driven who make all this possible.

"I'm under no illusions, and you shouldn't be, that our efforts will be anything more than a Band-Aid during brain surgery, a pebble in the ocean. I'm not here to bullshit you, Serene. But each one of these fools we take out saves the life of a girl in Rwanda or Slovenia or Costa Rica or Thailand. That's something to be proud of. We are not passive. We are not victims. We are holding men accountable when others won't. The women who are abused are the witnesses and the jury and the judge. We just carry out the sentence. Doesn't that sound good to you?"

Serene had no idea what to think of this long-winded monologue. Clearly the woman was crazy. "You are some kind of female vigilante?" Serene said.

Mildred didn't blink. "You can call it that if you want."

"Look," Serene said, "I'm not interested in being part of some conspiracy against men. I was searching for one of my students. Look at what that got me."

"In order to protect Alicia from her father you'll have to access a lot of lawyers," Mildred said. "I can fund that effort for you. In return, you will help me help others who are looking for stolen women."

"And," Serene said, trying to get a grip on her bewilderment, "what do *you* get out of this?"

"Justice," Mildred replied. "A little justice. I'll pay for everything, Serene. How does that sound to you?"

That was two years ago in the Bay Area. Now Serene was drying off in London before a trip to Berlin. She wasn't sure if she'd found justice, but she had found a purpose.

CHAPTER ELEVEN

WHO GON STOP ME

Vengeance is in my heart, death in my hand,
Blood and revenge are hammering in my head.
—William Shakespeare

Ice rolled out of bed at four a.m. Alone (as usual). Scared (which he didn't usually admit). Angry (as he often was). He was safe in Atlanta, but the city offered no respite from a heart filled with dread. Too much past. Too much blood.

Would he have to leave ATL too? He'd escaped New York years ago and found a haven. That hadn't lasted. Nothing would last. He knew that, but the alternative was a state-sponsored cage. Or he could just be dead. As disappointing as life was, death was an unknown he feared. He didn't see the faces of the men and women he'd killed in his dreams. Even Ice's subconscious was too damaged for empathy.

What scared him this night was that brief time in Virginia when he'd felt happy, justified, and stupidly safe.

With the cash he'd stashed, Ice had built a false identity, William Brown, and worked as a barber in the shop of old friend, Abdul Rahman, in a small southeast Virginia city. He'd developed this personal witness-protection program as the crack era was ending and folks who'd hired him were getting swept up in RICO investigations. The nature of crime in Brooklyn was shifting. His saving grace had been that he'd always been an independent operator and not a drug dealer. But no doubt his name had come up in connection with various transgressions. It was only a matter of time before someone used Ice's name to get their sentence shortened.

If he'd tried to make a deal and gone into witness protection, Ice would surely have been shipped to Oklahoma or Montana or some state where no one would know his hard, angular face. Ice knew he had to get away from New York but couldn't bear to move to a completely new world, even if that was truly the best way to stay safe.

Homeboy Abdul had opened a spot near a university with a strong Division II athletic program. That meant a lot of young brothers who had been recruited needed their hairstyles fly and facial hair sharp. Over time, the ballplayers brought their white teammates over to hang and, in turn, more white students and boosters followed. Performers who played the university talked it up to other groups coming across the Virginia/North Carolina border.

Ice was good with his hands, while his essential darkness was catnip to the kids who felt his "real G" quality—though any stories he told were "hypothetical" (wink, wink). Abdul, who'd converted to Islam in prison, was a versatile barber with a thick James Harden beard.

Ice soon developed a humorous story line that he'd share with new customers. "Just hear me out," he'd start. "A man walks in off the street, someone you've never met before, and a few minutes later you're trimming their mustache close enough to kiss them. You can feel their stress 'cause it jumps right on you. So not only do you get their hair on you, their stress gets on you too. I mean, the minute a man sits down in your chair you can tell by their skin how sick they are. You can see it in their perspiration and in their hair. Day after day, head after head, that adds up.

"Underneath my white jacket I wear thick clothes to work. Sweatshirts. Dungarees. When I get home I never wash my barber clothes with the rest of the wash. I even scrub the machine with a damp cloth when I'm through washing my barber clothes because of all the miscellaneous dust. You have to be careful 'cause people carry all kinds of viruses. But you can't kick a man out once he's in your chair—you have to deal with them then. Now, if I dealt with every head that walked in this shop, I could triple my money. If I didn't care what their skin looked like or how much of a hurry they were in, I could pull in as much as the man who owns this shop and works chair number three, a dude named Abdul.

"Abdul is good. Even in his little town, the man is a money machine. He won't pass up a head. He cuts it all: nigga, spic, wop, even Jews. He charges the Jews a little extra but he'll carve a Star of David in a Jew's head if they ask for it.

"But Abdul pays the price. He's had foot surgery. He sees a chiropractor for his back. From breathing in all that hair, Abdul has stomach problems.

"Right now, he's on the first vacation of his life and he only went up to New York to a barber-machine show where they're gonna demonstrate the world's fastest clippers. Otherwise, Abdul would be here right now, working six days a week, listening to men worry about their wives, their jobs, and how their daughter screwed up the gears on her new car. He lets his customers drop a load on his head even as he's cutting theirs. You see, cutting hair is slowly killing Abdul, youngbloods. But the man can't stop.

"I used to work like that, but not anymore. I learned my lesson. I get my feet rubbed with cocoa butter at this Asian massage parlor over in the next town. I put Johnson's baby powder in my shoes to absorb the sweat. I take breaks. I turn away anxious men. Unlike Abdul, I'm not gonna let this dangerous game kill me."

As amusing as Ice found his time at the barbershop, its popularity began attracting unwanted attention. A white cop named Bradley Bowen started coming in. Clearly the congregation of young black men at the shop had caused a lot of conversation around town. Bradley told Ice and Abdul not to worry; he wasn't there on official business. Bradley was, he said, "a frustrated" record producer who was obsessed with golden-age NYC hip hop like Wu-Tang, Rakim, and A Tribe Called Quest. "Law enforcement is a stopgap," the cop said. "I got a wife and kid so I needed a nine-to-five. But I love the music and the culture."

So, for Bradley, the camaraderie of men who'd survived the New York streets his idols rhymed about was more important than snooping too deeply into the background of the barbers. He figured that Abdul and Ice had done time but never gave a thought that his barber might be a cold-blooded contract killer (albeit retired).

One day, one of the ballplayers, having finished his mandatory English class, tossed a volume of Shakespeare's plays in the barbershop trash. Ice fished it out after work and began thumbing through it. For a Brownsville-educated man, Ice wasn't a bad reader, though old-time English was not his forte. He'd heard of Hamlet and Lady Macbeth, but most of his reading had been the *Daily News*.

Then, a bit of dialogue from Aaron in the play *Titus Andronicus* caught his eye: "*O how this villainy / Doth fat me with the very thoughts of it! / Let fools do good, and fair men call for grace; / Aaron will have his soul black like his face.*"

Ice grabbed a pen and went through the play, underlining Aaron's many vicious quips. He googled *Titus* and found a movie version of it on Hulu. There, Aaron was played by the light-skinned brother from NBC's *The Blacklist*. Since Ice had only skimmed the play, it wasn't until he saw the flick that he realized Aaron had a kid by the blond

Queen Tamora. This Aaron was a treacherous motherfucker! It was while watching the light-skinned brother playing Aaron that the first seeds of acting had been planted in Ice's head. He even began to see his story about Abdul as a dramatic monologue.

It was through *Titus Andronicus* that Ice began a relationship with Bradley Bowen's wife Tanya. She started bringing in their son, a tow-headed eight-year-old named Baker, who usually wanted a buzzy fade. One afternoon Tanya noticed the volume of Shakespeare's plays below a poster of Mike Tyson at Ice's station. She was shocked that the barber was reading the Bard. Turned out, Tanya had studied theater in college, and the idea of having someone, in this case her son's black barber, to talk to about Shakespeare was very exciting.

She began e-mailing him links to essays on *Titus* and then the play *Othello*, the description of which so offended Ice that he vowed never to read it or watch the movie version starring Laurence Fishburne. This communication with Tanya made him uncomfortable. He knew it was a seriously bad idea. Still, he was a straight man (one who had been traveling to Virginia Beach to enjoy escorts), so the prospect of having sex without paying for it was pretty tempting. He wasn't going to suggest it. But if the opportunity came up, Ice wasn't going to turn Tanya down.

One evening, she stopped by after closing. Abdul had just cut his last head and was leaving the sweeping-up to Ice, who was surprised that the boy wasn't with her. Turned out Bradley and Tanya had had a bit of a tiff and, as penance, Bradley had taken their son on a camping trip with A Tribe Called Quest as the soundtrack. Ice was rightfully nervous. The white wife of a local cop was alone with him at his place of business after hours: this sounded like the prelude to a lynching.

However, Tanya's mission wasn't a romantic one. Apparently, her husband wasn't so in love with hip hop that he'd lost his law enforcement instincts. He'd asked her to take a picture of Baker and "Willie" the next time she went to the barbershop. When Tanya asked why, Bradley said he wanted to upload the barbers' images to some national law enforcement and FBI databases. Tanya shared all of this information freely with Ice. At that moment, he knew his time in Virginia was up. So, when he reached out to hug Tanya in appreciation, he let his hands slide to her hips and let his lips find her neck. After they'd gotten creative with the swiveling barber's chair and Tanya had cried and laughed about cheating on her husband, Ice sat alone in the shop smoking a cigar, sad that he was going to have to move along.

Ice thought of Aaron's last lines in *Titus*: "*I am no baby, I, that with base prayers / I should repent the evils I have done: / Ten thousand worse than ever yet I did / Would I perform, if I might have my will; / If one good deed in all my life I did, / I do repent it from my very soul.*"

Ice had recently cried in acting class while performing a monologue based on Aaron's words in *Titus*. He thought it would scare the shit out of a roomful of sensitive artistic types. Instead, his soul opened up, making a mockery of his intentions. In Ice's head Aaron was defiant and proud, an empowered bloody bully. But uttering Shakespeare's words made him morose as he realized that Aaron was a weakling whose every act of evil was a struggle to overcome his impotence in a world that hated his guts.

When that realization hit Ice on that tiny stage before eight uncomprehending wannabe thespians, he sobbed so hard that snot bubbles popped out of his nose. He stumbled off, victim of an unwanted vulnerability stitched together from the frayed threads of his humanity.

Ice was crying again now, like a moaning bluesman, alone in the night in his ATL bedroom as he contemplated his next move.

CHAPTER TWELVE
BEST PART

Helen told Serene that the second *Bourne Identity* movie was shot at the Berlin hotel she was staying in. Serene hadn't seen the flick but would certainly order it on the flight home. The instructions had been slipped under her door the night before. It was chillier in Berlin than London, so she wrapped a scarf around her neck as she exited the hotel and made a right in the direction of the Cold War's infamous Checkpoint Charlie, where one could cross into Communist-controlled East Berlin. The checkpoint had been a place of espionage—people smuggled in the bottom of trucks, fake IDs, false beards, phony accents. Decades after reunification, the area was a testament to consumerism, with franchised retailers from around the globe lining the street. On this chilly morning, Starbucks beckoned Serene and she grabbed a chai latte before entering the Mitte U-Bahn station.

In the envelope were directions, train tickets, and a small map. These Liberator folks still used paper for a lot of business, being distrustful of the security of digital communications. "You should seem like a wandering tourist," Helen had advised, which would be easy since that's what she was. The U-Bahn train reminded her of the BART back in the Bay, but had longer cars connected by accordion-like sections that bent as the trains turned. The Berliners on the U-Bahn were a grim lot, not big on eye contact.

The massive Alexanderplatz station had the buzzy hum Serene recognized as big-city noise, but all the signs were in German and the wall's light-green tiles were more stylish than anything she'd experienced in US mass transit. Up some steps and past brightly lit shops, Serene followed the station signs to where the lockers were located.

After checking the hotel stationery for the right number, she stopped in front of locker 611. Looking over both shoulders, Serene punched in the code and the locker door popped open. Inside sat a lonely little white package, which she slipped it into her backpack before exiting through glass doors into the wide expanse of Alexanderplatz.

Like any good tourist, Serene wandered over to the World Clock, a sixteen-foot-high structure of concrete and metal with the names of cities around the globe inscribed around it. You could figure out the time in 148 major cities by looking at it. Between her days in London and this unexpected outing in Berlin, Serene suddenly felt like a citizen of the world. She had never felt like that when she was in the army. Back then everything was a reflection of US values and policy, with her uniform and her weapon defining every interaction wherever she was stationed.

That night, at Helen's suggestion, Serene took the U-Bahn over the Kreuzberg, a venerable neighborhood that had bordered the Berlin Wall before it was torn down. In the years since, Kreuzberg had become a popular late-night destination of bars and nightclubs. Serene wandered through the crowds, enjoying not understanding most of what was being said and admiring the tall, sturdy German men who checked her out.

Even though she had an extremely valuable piece of African history in her backpack, Serene felt relaxed. Unlike her work in the cesspool of human trafficking, there had been no asshole men, sellout women to confront, or damaged victims to comfort. Just open a locker and transport a piece of jewelry. The lack of complex human interactions was quite a respite.

Serene didn't get back to her room until three thirty a.m.—six thirty p.m. the previous evening on the West Coast. She called Arthur but he didn't pick up.

When she woke that afternoon, Serene found several missed calls on her phone from a number she didn't recognize. Helen picked up when she called back.

"There's been a change of plans," the older woman said in a shaky voice. "Soa, who was going to meet you today, was arrested yesterday evening in Belgium. So I think you should bring it back to the States with you."

"Is that wise?" Serene asked.

Helen spoke as if she were looking over her shoulder. "Just put it in your carry-on. If asked about it, it's a piece of costume jewelry you purchased from a Gypsy in Europe."

It was a joke of sorts. Helen forced a laugh, but Serene didn't bite. This was a responsibility she didn't need or want. A call to Mildred Barnes would be happening very soon.

"Okay," Serene said finally. "Do you want me to bring it anywhere in particular?"

"Take it with you to the Bay Area. I'll get back to you in a few days. And thank you."

"One more thing: Anika. Where is she?"

"We got her back home," Helen said. "I'll send you her phone number in a few days."

Serene hung up and then, reluctantly, unwrapped the package. She'd vowed not to take a look at it, not wanting any attachment to something so rare and valuable. But then it was in her hand—a gold medallion with a lion's visage on one side and a single green jewel on the other. Serene had never been to Africa but had the distinct feeling that this object would one day take her to the Motherland.

CHAPTER THIRTEEN
SKY WALKER

D's office was at 8570 Sunset, right down the block from the West Hollywood Equinox and a short stroll from the sidewalk cafés around Sunset Plaza. He'd thought about getting space at one of the WeWork spaces proliferating in town but they felt too collegiate and made him feel old. A music-publishing firm had recently cut its staff and had two extra offices, a shared conference room, and a reception area, so he rented there.

D was ensconced in one room with Marcy Mui, who sat at a smaller desk. In the other room was a management vet name Mal Maldron, who'd transitioned from the record business to brand development; and Ray Ray, whom D had known since he was an at-risk kid in Brooklyn, but who'd evolved into a digital music marketing whiz and a wannabe screenwriter.

D had first encountered Ray Ray and some of his associates at the turn of the century when they were about to set a sleeping homeless man on fire at the Canal Street subway station. After interrupting that activity (and whooping some stupid teenage ass), D had somehow become a mentor to Ray Ray, who, it turned out, lived in the same Brownsville housing project as D's family. Over the years, D nurtured Ray Ray's many interests and eventually helped him out when the kid enrolled in USC's film school. Until he sold his first screenplay or TV pitch, Ray Ray was toiling at D Management, giving his boss a connection to a black youth culture that he found harder to understand with every passing day.

There was also a desk in the space for D's old friend Al Brown, road manager extraordinaire, who lived in Florida and advised on all things Night. Walter Gibbs was D's undercover adviser and he had CAA whispering in his ear as well.

D's last New York office had served as home base for D Security, which had specialized in nightclub security. His crew had been NYC-born, streetwise, battle-tested, and fast with their hands. Back then, his staff meetings had been about VIP arrivals, drunks and druggies who were banned (unless they were VIPs), relations with the local precinct, security walk-throughs, and martial arts training. It was thoughtful work with a physical edge. The job was to not let people get hurt, to not hurt people, and, paramount, to not get yourself hurt.

Despite all the music and sexiness in any high-end club, there was always a chance you could be injured, and that gave every night an energizing edge. D's current profession, though much more lucrative, provided few potential jolts. Yeah, he could get sued for something silly by someone greedy. But that just wasn't the rush of possibly getting hurt. This LA team was a haphazard bunch—young and eager, experienced and tired, excited and anxious. It would only be a matter of time before he'd know if they were strong enough as a unit to keep him from drowning in Hollywood's deep waters.

Today D sat at the head of the conference table with Marcy, Mal, and Ray Ray scattered around him, and Al on speakerphone from Florida. A whiteboard behind him had a list of topics: Lil Daye, Mama Daye, Night, Dr. Funk, D's TV series, and new business. D gave updates on the various deals on the table for Lil Daye. McDonald's wanted him to do a commercial for their new breakfast menu. An energy drink wanted him to endorse a product called "Break of Daye." A deodorant company wanted Lil and Mama to post a series of Instagram pics of them using the product in their bathroom. "They are all well-paying," D said, "but none of them sound like what Vitamin Water did for 50 Cent or Cîroc for Diddy."

"I think all the ideas that pun on his name are corny," said Marcy.

"I agree," said Mal. "They all sound like those Taco Bell ads that helped Hammer kill his career."

"First of all, who's Hammer?" Ray Ray said, which made D laugh. Always good to have a historically clueless millennial in the house. "Anyway, niggas eat a lot of McDonald's. His audience would think he was getting paid to support a brand they relate to. Only people who don't eat at McDonald's are gonna be mad at that, and those folks aren't hard-core Lil Daye fans."

"Good points, everybody," D said. "I'll run them all by Lil Daye and let him know that he needs to be cautious about this pun shit. Too much is def a bad look. But then again, when Daye is your last name, you shouldn't be shy capitalizing on it."

Marcy gestured at the whiteboard. "So," she said with an edge, "are we managing his wife now too?"

"Well, we don't have any management papers on her. Her social media presence is off the chain. Maybe Lil and Mama could become the new Bey and Jay. Sounds like you have a problem with her."

"Her reputation is not good," Marcy said.

Ray Ray chimed in: "Yeah, I follow all the hip hop gossip sites and everyone down in ATL says she is a royal beeyatch."

"She sounds tailor-made for reality TV," Al said via speakerphone.

"Listen," D said, "if someone bites, we'll figure out a strategy. Right now, all we've been asked to do is help shop her to reality shows. She's already shot a couple of episodes so we won't have to beg for money. They'll see what it is and either buy it or not. And don't worry, Marcy, I won't have you babysitting Mama."

"Thank you," she responded. "I'm sure if I spent too much time with her, we'd come to blows."

"Yo, that would be lit," Ray Ray said. "A *WorldStar* exclusive for real."

"Okay," D said, "back to business."

The rest of the meeting was less flavorful as Night's Korean adventures and Dr. Funk's hologram appearances were old news. Marcy suggested mounting a Rock & Roll Hall of Fame campaign for Dr. Funk and Al thought they should have a separate call about it. The TV production company wanted to schedule a meeting with D to talk through their ideas for a series they were calling *Hip Hop Detective* ("That title is wack as hell," Ray Ray commented derisively), which he reluctantly agreed to.

"Any new business?" D asked finally, hoping to end this necessary but tedious gathering.

Mal said, "I got an inquiry from an old friend in Paris. He's looking for an American R&B/hip hop producer to work with a French female singer. It's a paying trip to Paris for a couple of weeks."

"I'll go," Ray Ray said with a grin. When everybody laughed at that, he added, "You all know my beats are fire."

"We've all heard your beats," Marcy countered with sass. "They won't be getting you a free trip to France."

"I cosign that," D said. "And on that note, this meeting has come to a close. Mal, let's get together later and see if we can find someone for that Paris gig."

"Night?" Mal said.

"I'm sure they'll want someone younger with a trap sound. Let's see if we can find someone in Lil Daye's camp we can submit."

Back in his office, D munched on a kale salad from the Sweetgreen downstairs and looked out across the city. From his window, LA's late-summer haze obscured Downtown's office towers. The vista didn't seem too magical this afternoon with the air thick with fumes. The sun was a blur through the airborne filth. Still, it was a view, one D had imagined having back in Brownsville, where from his family's apartment window all he could see were elevated subway tracks. That was literally a continent away. Or maybe just a phone call.

His cell played "Around the Way Girl." The name *Danielle Robinson*, the widow of his dead mentor Dwayne, appeared on the screen. With no introduction she said breathlessly, "I just met with a man from the FBI."

"Oh damn," D said with genuine surprise. "Are you okay? What did he want?"

"He was asking about your relationship to Dwayne. How close you two were and so forth."

"You think he's trying to figure out who killed Dwayne?"

"I would hope so," she said. "But he was real cagey. He was very interested in the book Dwayne was writing. He wanted to know why he was writing it, who knew he was writing it, and where he'd kept the manuscript. He was actually nice, but that doesn't mean I trusted him. D, you ought to be careful. The FBI are not good guys now just because Trump doesn't like them. They have never been the protector of black people. Dwayne is dead, they can't take anything away from him. But you have done so well for yourself, D. I don't want them to pull you down."

"I hear you, Danielle. I *will* be careful."

"You have met a lot of people in this world, D," Danielle said, sounding like a mother. "If you have any favors, use them and prepare yourself. Dwayne used to say the world can change with one phone call, and he was right."

D took this in. He was thankful that someone cared. "Danielle, I promise you I'll keep my eyes and ears open. Thank you so much for the heads-up."

There were calls he needed to make, meetings he needed to have, people who could be helpful in this troubling scenario. The one who'd be most useful was a man he detested. The devil's disciples were always well-connected.

CHAPTER FOURTEEN
GET YOU

After moving to LA, D had decided to be inside cars as little as possible. He'd rented a penthouse apartment in the Palazzo West complex, which was right across 3rd Street from the Grove outdoor mall and the adjacent Pan Pacific park, which had basketball courts, soccer fields, and baseball diamonds. On his side of 3rd was a Whole Foods and a CVS. In the other direction on La Brea was a twenty-four-hour Ralphs, perfect for late-night pickups.

So basically D just needed his Lexus for meetings in the Valley. Most of his daily needs were a few steps away. The Palazzo West had a pool (which was usually overrun by kids and pale girls in search of color) and a gym, but D preferred the Equinox a few blocks away on Wilshire. Though he did Uber to work on Sunset, most days he walked home, going down to Fairfax and then taking 3rd to his place.

It was remarkable how easy the transition had been from east to west. Every now and then, he'd visit his Aunt Sheryl and her son Walli out in Lancaster, but most of his life was lived in the Miracle Mile area of LA. Weekends he spent his time in either DTLA (Downtown LA), where most of the hippest clubs and progressive cultural institutions were located, or Echo Park, where he'd fallen in love with the Echoplex, which booked great NY DJs like Spinna or local star Rashida. Maybe, he thought, if all worked out, he'd buy a place in Echo Park. But for now, he was comfortable in his LA cocoon.

One part of D's new lifestyle that he hadn't relaxed into was the necessity of attending meetings at old Hollywood watering holes. He'd been to these places many times as a bodyguard and was always unpleasantly surprised at how elitist, snobbish, and clueless the people who made movies and TV were. It was an insular world of private schools, awards shows, and overpriced brunches, like the one he was on his way to now.

The Four Seasons Hotel on Doheny Drive had been a Hollywood power-breakfast spot for decades. Moguls of the silver screen and the analog recording studio had been meeting for early breakfast since the sixties. But just as CDs gave way to downloads, the Four Seasons had ceded much of its aura to Soho House and younger, more tech- and digital-friendly environments. So it was no surprise that Amos Pilgrim had asked D to meet him at eight thirty a.m. at this twentieth-century institution. Back when he was doing security, D had spent many days and nights in the Four Seasons, whisking celebs in and out of hotel rooms they shouldn't have been in and keeping the media at bay. The Four Seasons' security was some of the city's best, but D Security still had to do a lot of work keeping the celebrated from their most clueless impulses.

The Four Seasons Sunday brunch was famous for its vast supply of food. The weekday breakfast wasn't as bountiful, but it still made most others in town seem feeble. For years, this had been Amos Pilgrim's morning meeting location of choice. The businessman was notoriously crafty about the sequencing of his meetings. He knew how to keep enemies apart. He knew when to make sure people at odds could "accidentally" run into each other, and he would make sure two people who needed to know each other would cross paths. D figured there wasn't a breath Amos took that wasn't strategic, so he was curious who'd be sharing the man's booth when he arrived.

Amos was in his usual spot near the front of the dining room with his customary French toast, sunny-side-up eggs, and coffee in place. He was wearing an expensive-looking yellow zip-up sweater and a blue-faced Rolex. But, D thought, his eyes looked redder, the bags under them bigger, and his skin was dull. Time was taking its toll on this crafty man.

Across the table was a dark-brown beauty with short natural hair and the cheekbones of a model. She wore a sensible beige dress, an expensive gold watch, and bracelets. She was obviously a woman of class and means, though her brown skin made her seem ageless.

"D," Amos said as he approached the table, "I'm just finishing up here. Why don't you grab a plate at the buffet and then come back."

"No," the woman said firmly, "don't chase Mr. Hunter away like that."

"Oh," D said, flattered that she knew who he was, "that's all right, miss."

"Forgive my manners," Amos said. "D Hunter, this is Belinda Bowman."

She stood up to shake his hand and D was quite impressed with her curvy figure, which he hoped he had taken in without looking too predatory.

"I guess you might as well sit down," Amos said, though D was quite sure this introduction had always been his plan.

Belinda Bowman was an attorney who represented a gang of recording artists and actors, including a few of the featured players in *Black Panther*. Amos had met her fresh out of Howard University School of Law and had advised her in negotiating the politics of the Century City law firm where she worked. It quickly became clear to D that Miss Bowman's brown eyes were aimed at handling his future deals. She knew all about his Lil Daye deal and his other moves.

D had been using an LA law firm Walter Gibbs recommended and he was satisfied with them, though he hadn't yet made a personal connection with any of the partners. Moreover, Gibbs was seemingly an important client there, making D wonder whether any side deals were being cut. Amos wouldn't have made this "accidental" hookup happen if Belinda Bowman wasn't good. (Amos didn't believe in rewarding black mediocrity.)

"Do you handle any of Amos's business?" D asked.

She said, "My firm does, so I get to dip my fingers into his affairs."

"If I let her, she'd renegotiate every damn thing I do," Amos said. "But she's built up a nice client list of her own. She doesn't really need an old man's business."

Belinda shook her head. "Right. Like you aren't still doing business all over town." Then she reached into her handbag and pulled out a business card, handing it to D. "One way or another, I'm sure we'll do business." She gave Amos a kiss on the cheek and shook D's hands vigorously before leaving.

D tried not to be caught checking out the attorney's butt when she walked away.

"Smart woman," Amos said.

"Seems like it," D responded.

Then there was a pause as both men geared up for the uncomfortable conversation to come.

"So," Amos began, "you can imagine I was surprised to hear from you."

"I'm sure you know it's a conversation about trouble."

"I'm gonna assume that this has nothing to do with that rapper you're working with in Atlanta, or Night, or anything else aboveground?"

"Yeah," D said, "it's underground shit."

Amos stared at D, evidently displeased. "If you'd made that clear, we could have met at my office."

"Well," D said, "in case I'm being watched, I wanted it to look like a social meet-up, not business."

"Okay, James Bond, we're here now."

"There's an FBI agent asking questions about me back in Brooklyn. I just need some background on the agent, how much of a priority I am for them, and if this guy is freelancing or on some serious FBI-sanctioned investigation. You know a lot about freelancing agents."

Amos raised his voice: "Stop being so fucking coy and tell me what the fuck this is about."

"Eric Mayer," D said evenly. "His body was found in Jamaica Bay."

Amos thought a moment, then asked, "What is this agent's name and what is he asking about?"

D related what he'd been told by Ice and what Fly Ty had heard. Amos ate his French toast slowly, not speaking. D waited, letting this power broker connect all his internal dots.

Finally Amos said, "Do *not* meet with this agent Conrad until you hear from me. You hear me?"

"I'm sitting right here."

"When Mayer disappeared, I knew he had it coming," Amos said quietly. "You know how he turned on me. Someone was gonna take him out. I knew it wouldn't be me—I don't do that kind of thing. But I know in Brooklyn there are people who would cut throats for a quarter. People who'd be friends of yours. But I never made a big deal out of it 'cause that shit never splattered on me."

So Amos knew D had been involved in Mayer's death. How *much* he knew, D didn't care to ask. So he just puffed his chest and spat back, "But you did smell of it."

Amos wasn't feeling D's smug response. "Motherfucker, I could make a phone call and you'd be bound, gagged, and stomped into the size of a blueberry. Shit, I wouldn't need to call—I could just text."

D knew this was true but he wasn't there to back down. "You have enough on your conscience, Amos," he said, trying to sound conciliatory though his tone was severe. "I lost someone I loved in that shit, so don't threaten me. Besides, the world is a different place. Bill Cosby isn't America's father. Jesse Jackson can barely speak. There are crazy people talking about LeBron being better than Jordan. Amos, you don't wanna join that list of fallen black gods of America. You have friends in high and low places. Find out what you can and we'll talk. Thanks for the sit-down."

D got up quickly and felt Amos's eyes on his back, hoping he'd do what D asked and not text the wrong people.

CHAPTER FIFTEEN
WHITE MEN IN SUITS

D had no idea there was an area in Los Angeles named Highland Park. It was farther east than he'd been in the City of Angels. Leave it to Night to find new territory to explore. They hadn't seen much of each other in the last eight months between D's business building and Night's work in Korea. His old friend seemed to have (finally) beat down his addiction demons and even had a girlfriend he hadn't met at a club, bar, or backstage. Night had met Mina at Crossroads, a vegan restaurant in town, and they were now living together in Silver Lake. So now Night rarely came west of Hollywood and was mostly working out of a small studio called the Red Gate off Echo Park Avenue.

The Red Gate was next to a drive-through Starbucks. There was an actual red gate in front, through which you entered into a small studio whose decor looked like it hadn't been updated since 1993. Felt like the bar in *Pulp Fiction*. D was waiting for Marsellus Wallace to come out from the back talking shit. Night sat on a bruised-red leather sofa eating vegan tacos with a Mexican American engineer named Sam.

After their greetings D observed, "This spot was probably retro before retro knew it was retro."

"Yeah," Night said with a chuckle, "they can't even auto-tune in this motherfucker—right, Sam?"

Sam agreed: "This joint is digital optional, analog dedicated."

There were beat-up Persian rugs on the floors, lots of leather (and pleather) sofas and chairs, curvy eighties lamps, and bit of analog equipment (mixers, stereos, vinyl) stacked along the walls for atmosphere. It was a recording studio that time forgot, which suited Night just fine.

"I wanted you to hear this music in the right environment," he said, "not on some Beats By Dre earphones while lounging in your ATL Jacuzzi."

"Okay," D said, "you got me out in the ass end of LA. There's more vintage boutiques out here than luxury-car dealerships, so I know you have some throwback shit for me."

"Throwback," Night replied, "and throw-forward. I've realized that you shouldn't spend more than 10 percent of your time worried about what people think of you on social media, people who never did a creative thing in their lives except make up a Twitter password."

"Okay, my suddenly wise friend, what have you been doing with the other 90 percent of your time?"

"Eating. Sleeping. Fucking. Creating. But not in that order."

"I've seen Mina, so I know in what order you mean." The old friends shared a laugh and then D said, "Okay, my man. Okay. You've been thinking a lot about your next moves?"

"About time, right? I spent, what, thirty-eight years just doing shit? I was like an animal—all basic instincts, no reflection, introspection, or inspection of self. Time is precious."

"You made some good music in your youth, Night. Enduring shit, actually. 'Black Sex' is a classic, no doubt about it."

"I didn't do enough, though," Night said. Even frowning he still had the dark Gable looks that made him a sex symbol. "You see Bey? She outworked me. She outworked *all* of us. She wasn't precious about a sound. She was the product and she used whatever sound or image or book or whatever was hot to *stay* hot. While I was playing with my dick or having someone else play with it, Bey was at work. Like her husband said, *Can't knock the hustle.*"

"Okay, Mr. Hard Work. Mr. Focus. Mr. Nine-to-Five. What ya got for me to hear?" D asked.

Night motioned to Sam, who was now sitting in the small control room. Music flowed out of the Red Gate's speakers. There was a touch of auto-tune on Night's voice, but the track wasn't a slave to the twenty-first century. There were a few Prince-like keyboard horn patches and it sounded like he'd done some kind of digital treatment on an 808. The keys were old Hohners and Wurlitzers and the guitars were as busy as James Brown's backside. It felt funky and ominous, like an outtake from *There's a Riot Goin' On.* Night's vocals were as angry as D had ever heard them. No song titled "White Men in Suits" was getting programmed next to Justin Bieber anyway.

Singing hymns to property,
Ringing bells to poverty,
They're all just white men in suits.
White men in suits, white men in suits.

Living lives of luxury,
Drowning in designer things,
Laughing from penthouse peaks,
They're all just white men in suits.
White men in suits, white men in suits.

They stand on legal steps,
While taking illegal steps,

They talk of mortality,
When they just don't want you free.
They're just white men in suits,
White men in suits, white men in suits.

Where do you go? Where do you flee?
When the doors are closed and the jackals roam free,
They don't need masks to hang us all from trees,
And charge us with a fee.
They're just white men in suits.
White men in suits, white men in suits.

When the keyboard horns faded and the beat disappeared, Night turned to D and said, "That is a long way from 'Black Sex,' right?"

"Absolutely," D said.

"So, what do I do with it?"

"That song right there is what the Internet was made for. Lemme make up a release plan and bring it to you."

"You sure you have time now that you're trappin'?"

"That's money, Night," D said. "This is love." He reached over and gave his old friend a hug. "Now, nigga, I hope you have some kind of new love song somewhere so I can get you some dates in Europe after the Trump Twitter storm behind this shit."

Night cracked up. "All right, D. Chill out."

D loved "White Men in Suits," but he knew it was going to be one more ball to uneasily juggle in the months ahead.

CHAPTER SIXTEEN
LET ME DOWN

D hiked up to a landing at Runyon Canyon and was sitting on a bench looking down at Los Angeles spread out in front of him. His legs were tired but his lungs were happy. Filling them with the city's slightly gray oxygen still beat walking on the Equinox treadmill and being barraged by TV screens. There were two cute ladies taking selfies as they sat on the edge of the hill. A man in awfully tight leggings served treats to his shaggy dog. A gay couple sat on the other side of the bench talking about a horrible boss.

Speaking of bosses, D knew messages from the East Coast were already pouring in. He reached into his backpack and reluctantly pulled out his Samsung. There were a lot of fresh missives but one in particular caught his eye: *LIL DAYE! WE MET IN ATLANTA.* He opened up the message:

Mr. Hunter, my name is Dorita Johnson. I met you at Magic City with Lil Daye, who I have been in an intimate relationship with for two years and seven months. We have expressed our love for each other many times. I was going to have a baby for him when I got pregnant but he wanted me to wait and I did. That was very painful for me, but for Lil Daye I did it. He said it wasn't time and that I had to protect him until he was clear of his wife. He said he would marry me. He doesn't say that now that he's making big money. I *didn't want to hurt him but he has hurt me to my core. I have text messages from him and videos of his manhood. I know the code to his home and his wife's dress size. I am not asking for much. I just need $150,000 right now to help me out. I gave him everything and he has left me alone and with nothing. I won't cause him any trouble. I am not out to hurt him. I would never want to hurt him. He hasn't kept his promises to me and that's hurtful.*

D sighed deeply. He remembered Dorita from that night at Magic City. He figured much of what she wrote was true. If she said she'd had a baby by Lil Daye, he would have understood. But he was surprised to hear that Lil Daye had urged her to have an abortion and knew that information would be a bad look on black Twitter. D had no idea how Mama Daye would view this. She had to know Lil Daye had women, but that thing about knowing Mama Daye's dress size was explosive.

Now it was really time for D to earn his manager's fee and be the guy who makes bad things go away. Before he did any heavy strategizing, however, he called Lil Daye, left a message, and then sent a text: *Dorita Johnson just e-mailed me.*

He sat on the bench watching people absorb the LA vista as he awaited a response. Two minutes later, his phone rang. "So," D said by way of greeting, "how do you want me to handle this?"

"You don't. I got this." It sounded like Lil Daye wanted that to be the last word.

"Really? She wouldn't have sent this to me if you two were getting along. It sounds like she wants me to negotiate a truce."

"Dorita is a personal problem of mine," Lil Daye said emphatically. "I'm sorry she got at you but I just want you focused on making deals and expanding my brand. This is some ATL shit, so I'm gonna handle it an ATL way."

"That makes me nervous."

"We making money moves, D, and we gonna keep making money moves. I ain't gonna endanger my cash flow for some bitch. All right?"

Lil Daye danced around the specifics of what *an ATL way* meant before he got off the phone, leaving D peering out at the city with very different eyes than just fifteen minutes earlier. Rap stars were not known for having good relationship judgment. Leaving this in Lil Daye's hands sounded like a fast track to the penitentiary. That thought was D's cue to head back down Runyon Canyon and get to work.

When D picked up his phone at seven a.m. the next morning, he was expecting a text from New York. A product manager at Universal Music Group wanted to go over the track listings and credits for a vinyl release of Lil Daye's last LP. Though it wouldn't mean much to Lil Daye's profitability, D thought a vinyl release would give the project a bit of old-school class.

But the text wasn't from New York. Or maybe it was. He didn't recognize the number, which had an 814 area code. Whoever it was didn't leave their name either, not that it really mattered. The mystery of the sender was dwarfed by the impact of the link. It was a *New York Times* article headlined, "ENTERTAINMENT MOGUL ACCUSED OF SEXUAL ASSAULT: Entrepreneur Walter Gibbs Abused Seven Women."

D sat up in his bed, the morning LA sun flowing in around his window shades. He'd known Gibbs since his days as a doorman at Manhattan nightclubs, back when New York was hip hop "every day, that's my word," and Jay-Z was sharing champagne "with six model chicks, six

bottles of Cris'." Gibbs had been a role model for D as he moved from
hired beef to talent manager. The businessman had been an adviser on
most of D's deals.

Gibbs had always been aggressive with women and, in D's eyes,
successfully so. D thought back to blurry nights at Lotus when he'd
pulled Gibbs out of the ladies' room on several occasions. Had those
girls been willing or just stoned out of their minds? Had Gibbs's hands
under tables been seduction or a prelude to rape?

Damn, D thought.

He texted Gibbs: *You see the Times article?*

Four seconds later, Gibbs replied, *Come over.* The man had been an
early riser ever since he, along with half his generation of hip hop folk,
had relocated to Los Angeles. He often meditated after waking up. Afterward, he was usually doing business calls to New York by eight a.m.
Gibbs's lifestyle was a long way from nineties New York when rappers,
models, and sundry creatures of the night roamed the Big Apple.

According to the *Times* article, it was precisely those nights that
had Gibbs in trouble. One woman accused him of forcing her into oral
sex in the back of an SUV. Another said he'd made her jerk him off
at the Russian bathhouse on East 10th Street. The most serious was a
model who claimed to be underage when they got busy at his Tribeca
loft. There were some familiar names in the piece. D recognized the
name of an aspiring publicist–turned–advertising executive from back
in the day. But thankfully, most of them he didn't know. As he read
the piece, they seemed united—they all testified that the spirit of the
#MeToo movement had emboldened them to speak out.

As D got dressed, he recalled how tight Dwayne Robinson had been
with Gibbs. Both their careers went back to the days when hip hop was
called rap and it was an underdog movement, not a billion-dollar busi-

ness. Thinking about Dwayne, his unfinished book, and the legacy of nineties violence, D realized that the past was inescapable and that the excesses of youth could calcify into middle-aged scars.

D's last visit to Gibbs had left a lingering bad taste in his mouth. It had been November 8, 2016. Gibbs had organized an election-night soiree which, as the electoral college results came in, transformed into a wake. The electoral college had made a raging, narcissistic reality-show star and debt-ridden businessman into president of the United States.

People muttered to themselves. A woman cried in a corner and sipped a lot of red wine. A Jewish man raged at God out by the pool. Everyone in that room was either a Democrat or Independent and all had, to varying degrees, supported Hillary.

Gibbs had sat there in front of his huge screen and wondered if the new commander in chief was still open to cutting deals. Gibbs knew the man had no principles so, in his opinion, the Dems could still find common ground. His naive optimism was a holdover from those nights when the then-young real estate mogul had been open to anything. Trump and Gibbs had partnered on a couple of small ventures in Atlantic City back when that was the new promised land. They hadn't spoken in years but Gibbs wondered if maybe some of that old friendship still had value.

D handled security at so many parties where the then-dark-haired businessman would sit in banquettes with Gibbs and others, talking about deals, models, and where to live in the Hamptons. That was just before he discovered that public racism was an effective marketing strategy and called for the lynching of the Central Park Five. No amount of evidence that those five boys from Harlem were not rapists ever got him to apologize. In his bottomless desire for acceptance, Trump's hip hop hangs had been replaced by the embrace of the right and a different brand of predatory capitalism. Needless to say, Gibbs and his old buddy never rekindled their friendship. Who needed hip hop connections when you had the power to launch nuclear warheads?

Gibbs lived in Beverly Hills, not far from Sunset Boulevard, in a house protected from the street by tall hedges decorated with roses and gardenias. There were several cars parked along the curb so D had to drive up the block to find a spot. He was about to text for the code to the gate hidden by the hedges, but then saw that it was open. So was the large brown front door. The interior hallway was dotted with art (paintings by Clemente and Basquiat). Other than the artwork, the place had the feel of a very fancy Asian-fusion restaurant. From the stairs, he heard CNN droning on, though its sound was somewhat drowned out by live voices. A woman's voice was the loudest.

"She was a ho from way back. Everybody knew that," she said matter-of-factly.

When D climbed the steps and entered the master bedroom, he found Gibbs sitting in bed, glasses on his forehead, iPhone in his hand, and laptop by his side. Scattered around the room on chairs and cushions were Gibbs's personal assistant Rachel; his boy from way back, Stace; TV producer and one-time employee, Sunny; his partner in several ventures, Ben Wilson; and a young attractive Asian woman whose dazed expression made D think she was Gibbs's current girlfriend.

Dominating the conversation was Sunny, a jack-of-all-trades entertainment business figure who'd done publicity and talent booking, and had been in Gibbs's circuit for decades. It was her voice that D had heard from downstairs.

"I never did like that bitch," she said before she noticed D, then turned to him and asked, "You ran through her too, didn't you?"

"No," D said evenly, "I did not."

"Then you must have been the only man in Manhattan who didn't."

Deciding to ignore this whole conversation, D turned to Gibbs and asked how he was feeling.

"Well, my life isn't over," Gibbs replied, "but other than that, I don't feel too good."

Usually animated by the joy of deal making, spiritual practice, or charming women, Gibbs now appeared low-energy, like an oven waiting to fully heat. Thankfully, he was not teary-eyed, but the sadness in the room was like a weight on him. It was weird to see Gibbs so down. Despite all this, his natural spark had been burning brighter since he'd started meditating. Gibbs had grown stronger, mentally and spiritually, and had developed a genuine heal-the-planet attitude.

The last few months, as D grew his management business, the two had mostly communicated via text and e-mail. Gibbs had a million projects cooking, but always took time to help D with deal points. D felt guilty that they hadn't hung out before he left for Atlanta. Whatever rush that negotiating used to bring was, while not gone forever, permanently altered. Gibbs's life would now be defined as pre- and postaccusation. The same for those around him. The people in this room were his friends and business partners. D wondered how many would still call him that in six months.

"You hurt your back today?" D asked, motioning to a back brace lying on the bed.

"Nawn," Gibbs said, "last week. I really can't get around too well. When God shits, it splatters everywhere." He flashed that salesman's smile but there was no mirth behind it, just the shadow of a buried joke. "It ain't a shock," he went on. "Ever since the Harvey Weinstein thing, I've had people claiming I bent them over tables at my office or grabbed their pussy. One of the girls wanted $300,000 for her 'church.' When I said it didn't happen, she went away until today."

"When did she say that happened?" D asked.

"Nineteen fucking ninety-three. I never touched her and would never have touched her. D, you know how I roll."

"But Gibbs," Sunny said, "you did manipulate a lot of women."

"This woman here said she felt threatened and afraid," Stace said, glancing down at the newspaper.

Sunny shot back, "She sucked his dick out of fear? Please. She sucked his dick to help her career."

Gibbs didn't like the implication that he got laid for status alone. "Well, maybe she just liked me."

"So," D asked, "none of these women thought you'd do something for them?"

"I didn't like Harvey Weinstein," Gibbs replied. "I didn't like Bill Cosby. I'm not them and I will not accept being lumped in with them. I had consensual sex with a lot of women. Period. These seven women are wrong. They are caught up in the moment. They are having second thoughts. Maybe I didn't end things right. I dunno. I know what I did and didn't do. But okay, they may remember things differently."

"What's our next move?" Sunny asked.

"I have a call with my lawyer and publicist soon," Gibbs said. "They are drafting a statement." He was clearly trying to hold it together, but there was no doubt he was shaken to his core.

"Most of them are looking for a payday, right?" said Sunny. Of all the folks in the room, she was the only one who didn't sound defensive. She had a high opinion of Gibbs and a low opinion of other industry women.

"You need to hire Trump's attorney," Stace said. "He's obviously an expert at getting NDAs signed."

"Shit," Gibbs said, "Trump was there when I met half these women."

"Didn't you hook him up with hos?" Sunny asked.

"Oh . . ." D said, for a moment excited at the prospect of implicating the president. But reality set in quickly. "I wish you could go there. You know a lot about him."

"I do," Gibbs said softly. "But being linked with him wouldn't help me. It would open the door to more bullshit."

D could see where this was going. He wanted to be loyal to Gibbs, but he also realized there were things about his friend's behavior he didn't know and never would. Gibbs had been too good of a friend to abandon. D would never do that. But if he was going to be useful, he knew he had to be clear-eyed and uncomfortably truthful. He said to Gibbs, "Can I offer a bit of advice?"

"Why the fuck you think I invited you over?"

"Take this L with grace," D said. "Do not call these women liars. Your attorneys are gonna say, *Don't admit anything.* Maybe from a legal viewpoint they are right. But in the real world of public opinion and Twitter, you can't win by attacking them."

Gibbs looked D in the eye and said, "I did nothing wrong."

"But these women say you did. In this moment in history, being a powerful, rich man is not an asset. All the advantages it gave you before are now liabilities if you flex on these women the wrong way—"

"I hear what you're saying, D. But I am not a bad person and won't let myself be defined as one by standing back and being silent."

At that moment, the awaited text from the Universal product manager hit D's phone. He stepped off into a corner to read it, though really he was just looking for a graceful exit. The mood was like a wake, except that the body was alive. A few men D had encountered over the years had been accused of sexual misconduct pre-Weinstein. D's days running a security company and being a private bodyguard had put him in contact with stars of all perversions. Drug use? He looked the other way. Run-ins with the law? He tried to keep them out of jail. Underage girls or violence against women? He stopped it when he could and quit when he couldn't. It was easy to become an accessory to a crime.

As Gibbs and his crew continued their conversation, D wondered if he'd been an enabler, protecting men from little crimes that later gave way to true evil. Had he just been a tool in helping rich people exploit poorer folks? Not what he wanted to contemplate at nine in the morning.

As D was about to exit the room, Gibbs called him over to the bed and whispered, "Stay my friend, D."

"Don't doubt that," D responded. "Don't ever doubt that."

CHAPTER SEVENTEEN
PRETTY WINGS

D rarely traveled out to Malibu. It was a part of the whole LA entertainment business lifestyle he'd yet to explore. So when R'Kaydia Lelilia Jenkins invited him to a lunch at Soho's Little Beach House in Malibu, he said, "Of course." He was a Soho House member, but the general membership didn't apply out at the location by the ocean. You needed a special deal to gain entry and, apparently, D hadn't quite made the cut. There were so many levels to the game out here.

He knew LA was a town defined by access. What meetings, parties, lunches, etc., you had access to meant what possible deals or projects could you stumble into. To really prosper in LA you needed a web of connections, a web that had never included very many people of color. Quincy Jones had the town wired for decades. D's sometimes-partner, sometimes-antagonist Amos Pilgrim had been an African American inside man since the days they'd been called *Negro*. These two were the rare legacy men of color in this dreamscape metropolis.

R'Kaydia had married into Malibu via the film producer Teddy Tapscott, but she'd also had her own serious Silicon Valley connections before the wedding. She was building a brand-new Hollywood mix of music, celebrity, and twenty-first-century tech savvy. Black Twitter loved R'Kaydia's swag. White men loved R'Kaydia's looks. You didn't need much more than that to make money these days. Her relationship with D had been rocky at times. He didn't find her quite as sexy as she required, which irritated her. Plus, despite working together on the hologram deals for Dr. Funk and Night, she felt D wasn't giving her the proper respect as a businesswoman.

On the ride out to Malibu, D wondered if he was a male chauvinist. Had he seen too many groupies in his bodyguard days to take businesswomen seriously? Instead of truly embracing R'Kaydia, he'd kept her at arm's length. If she'd been a black man making these moves, wouldn't they have been closer? Maybe R'Kaydia's combination of beauty and brains *did* scare him. Perhaps, if he was really being honest with himself, he just resented the fact that she was married to a white man.

The Little Beach House was on the left side of the Pacific Coast Highway coming from Santa Monica and shared a parking lot with Nobu, a combo of moneyed watering holes for the pretty. After he checked in, D walked past a long bar up a staircase lined with myriad paintings and photographs along the white wall. On the second floor, he found a dark wooden deck to his right. Sitting at the table nearest the ocean was R'Kaydia, giving D serious Audrey Hepburn vibes with large oval sunglasses, large yellow hat, sundress, sandals, red purse, and matching belt. She was sipping white wine and gazing at the waves rushing against the beach below. When she smiled, it was a movie-star moment. Her teeth were so white that D had to squint.

"D," she said, standing and giving him a hug, "so nice of you to come out here to see me." Her perfume was honeysuckle with a hint of ginger. D took it in before sitting down. "How was Atlanta?"

She sat forward in her chair as D talked about Lil Daye, trap music, and the general ATL vibe. Her brown eyes were lighter than D remembered and danced with amusement as he described the night at the strip club with Lil Daye. Talking with the black Audrey Hepburn about trap music and pole dancers by Malibu's beach was about as weird as it gets, D thought.

R'Kaydia pulled out her iPad and showed D visuals for the next phase of her company's evolution; they were investing in virtual-reality locations around the country, including comedy VR experiences. It was all cool, but also stuff R'Kaydia could have sent links to. He figured there was more to this meeting than hyping him on her latest tech play.

Finally, R'Kaydia said, "You know your friend Walter is an asshole, right?"

"I knew he was aggressive with women," D said carefully. "But what he's being accused of I never saw."

"That doesn't mean it didn't happen," she replied.

"No," he said quickly. "It doesn't mean that. But it's hard for me to digest. I know of a few of those women from back in the day. A couple were class acts. A few weren't."

R'Kaydia sighed. "What's a class act to you, D?"

Damn. D knew he was already in too deep. "A woman who can be flirty and sexy," he said, "and still keep her poise and not get played by the men on the scene."

"So," she leaned toward him, staring hard, "you believe these classy women more than you believe the nonclassy women?"

"I didn't say no stupid shit like that, R'Kaydia. What goes on behind closed doors only has two witnesses. So I don't really think you know anyone sexually if you haven't slept with them. But I can't lie, it hurts to see all Gibbs accomplished, all the good he did do, obliterated. So lemme ask you: did Gibbs cross the line with *you?*"

"He said some slick shit to me once or twice, but if he'd touched me I would have snapped his little dick with pliers. I don't have a girlfriend in this town he hasn't tried to make a move on."

"It's hard to get a grown-ass man to change his behavior," D said, "especially one with more money than you. You can offer advice. You can make comments. You can tell him calm the fuck down. But he's gonna do what he's gonna do. I wish he could have found and stayed in a healthy relationship. I'm not sure he'd know one if he had it. But hey, I'm not sure I would either. I mean, who am I to advise anybody on relationships?"

"Well, this is a new world, D," R'Kaydia admonished. "Women's voices are being heard no matter how powerful the man is or how uncomfortable it makes you or any other man feel."

Now it was D's turn to sigh. He looked out at the ocean for a moment, thinking before speaking. "Listen, when I did security I had to toss many a predatory fuckboy out on his ass. I know many men ain't shit. I know that. You see people at night high off drugs and money and you see the ugliness bold as fuck. But this Gibbs thing has me feeling some kind of way and it will for a long time. He's done me so many solids over the years; he'll never be a villain to me—even if people try to tell me he should be."

"Listen," R'Kaydia said, soft but stern, "be his friend—he's gonna need them. But let me give you a bit of advice: don't get caught out there sayin' he didn't do this or that. You may even believe it. But know that people are keeping score. Don't get caught on the wrong side of history."

"I hear you." D was looking in her direction but also right through her, his insides a jumble of despair.

R'Kaydia spoke to him like he needed to be snapped out of a trance: "I'm not telling you this just because I like you. I want you to be able to help us both make money. I know Gibbs's role in your business career—adviser and deal consultant. Well, he's gonna be busy trying to save his own ass. You'll need new friends."

"Aren't we friends already?"

"We get along well enough, I think," she said with a sly smile. "We've made each other money. I live in the tech world and that's where the real money is nowadays. You get along well with talent. Our skill sets complement each other. Our agendas match up."

That's cold-blooded, D thought, *but on point too.* He said, "Sounds like you're proposing a partnership."

"Not a formal one. Not yet."

"What's your husband think of this idea?" *Oh damn,* he immediately thought, *why did I go there?* He could feel her writing *Male Chauvinist* on his forehead with her eyes.

"I give *him* advice, D," she said with a bit of steel. "He doesn't give *me* advice. I do what makes sense. A stronger connection between you and me makes sense. Think about it."

A woman D didn't recognize approached the table—thin, white, blond, and dressed tastefully, including the big rock on her left hand. She and R'Kaydia began chatting about a charity event the following week in the Pacific Palisades.

D's gaze drifted out to the Pacific. In the distance he saw two dolphins dancing like children in the waves. *A good life,* he thought.

CHAPTER EIGHTEEN

LAKE BY THE OCEAN

After dining with R'Kaydia, D drove down to Santa Monica and posted up on a bench overlooking the Pacific Coast Highway. The ocean was in the near distance and the Santa Monica Pier to his left. Homeless men wandered around talking to themselves. There were portly tourists taking selfies with the Pacific as the backdrop. Teens on electric scooters zoomed by, heedless of pedestrians. A seagull hung over D for a moment and then, after some deliberation, decided not to dump on his head.

The sun was slowly lowering and giving off a nice wave of heat as the ocean breeze made sweating impossible. In an hour or so, he'd need to button up his jean jacket and grab a cup of tea on the 3rd Street Promenade. But at this moment, with his arms hanging over the top of the bench, his legs spread wide, his eyes closed, he felt an especially pleasing breeze and contemplated that perhaps he should just join the active homeless population in Santa Monica and set himself up on this nicely curved piece of green-painted metal. D smiled as two seagulls danced a duet in the distance against the light-blue sky.

Whenever D questioned his new life in Los Angeles (which was often), he came out to the Pacific Ocean and the city's sins were redeemed. D had considered getting a place in Santa Monica, Venice, or another ocean-side community, but ultimately decided against it. He didn't want to become immune. No way did he want the calmness that overtook him on his visits to the ocean to become commonplace. He'd found only a few things in his life that made him feel this good. He didn't want to OD on it.

With his head clear and his breath slow, D knew it was time to turn his attention to more unpleasant matters. He felt like he'd done his due diligence with Lil Daye. Like a lot of poor black kids in Atlanta, Daye (real name Javon Dillard) had been in and out of juvenile detention centers for much of his adolescence. He hadn't grown up in a trap house, but many of his friends had. Bits and pieces of that lifestyle filled out his rhymes.

Far as D was concerned, that background just made Daye another young black boy in a country that viewed them as a) cannon fodder, b) athletic entertainment, c) walking nightmares, d) born to be jailed, or e) valueless. It was D's opinion that no matter what you thought about today's rap as art, its existence was justified because it empowered the hungry in ways few avenues of American capitalism did.

D hadn't looked too deeply into Ant's background, an oversight that Ice's cautionary words made him regret. He knew Ant had been part of Lil Daye's camp since his first tracks blew up on SoundCloud, serving as an adviser, bodyguard, and financial backer. But if Ice knew about Ant, it meant he might have some bodies on his résumé, and that was not a good look.

Down in Atlanta, Ant had projected low-intensity hate toward D, though he'd never actually said anything threatening. It was just a vibe of discomfort. Maybe he was disappointed that he couldn't make the moves D could. Maybe he was insecure that he'd reached the ceiling of his usefulness and that translated into hostility toward D. If Ant actually owned a piece of Lil Daye, then D was making him money. But foolishness often led people to work against their self-interest. The problem was that aside from Ice, whom he didn't know how to get in contact with, his only other real contact in Atlanta was old-ass Fly Ty Williams, who didn't have any idea who ran ATL trap houses.

The twists and turns in Lil Daye's love life were, thankfully, far less complex. D had already gotten interest from VH1, Lifetime, and Andy Cohen over at Bravo regarding a possible reality show for Mama Daye. Her social media profile was robust and she seemed sassy enough to become the next Cardi B. It wasn't D's cup of culture, but *Love & Hip Hop* had been on since 2011 and you could monetize like crazy off that exposure.

As for that Dorita, he'd passed that e-mail on to Lil Daye and would wait for his feedback. D wanted to be a manager, not a fixer. He was no Michael Cohen. He could protect people, but cutting deals with mistresses was not why he'd become a talent manager. Perhaps he was being too precious. If he wanted to make big money in this game, it would be hard to keep his hands clean. He'd wait a few more days before checking in with Lil Daye to see how he'd played it.

Besides, he had his own dirt. Somewhere across the country, in his hometown next to the Atlantic, there was an FBI agent asking questions about the biggest mistake of his life. *The past is never gone. Revenge exposes your morality. Youth haunts middle age like the devil rules hell.* With his mind focused on those thoughts, all the good vibes on that bench melted away.

D was about to walk over to the promenade when his Samsung buzzed. He didn't recognize the number, and after having picked up Ice's call in Atlanta, he planned to stick to his don't-answer-unknown-numbers policy. *If they really want me,* D thought, *they will let me know.* Ten seconds later, a text popped up:

Mr. Hunter, Samuel Kurtz of Diversified International Brands would love to meet with you in Los Angeles this week. My name is Ingrid Britton. Please call me so we can set up the meeting. Good day.

D did a quick Google search and found that DIB was a multinational corporation with extensive holdings in luxury brands and spirits. Kurtz himself was a billionaire. He sounded like a man D should be calling back. But before he moved on to new business, a call to his past was in order.

After they'd gotten beyond greetings, D asked Serene Powers, "Where exactly are you these days, my friend?"

"I'm back home now," she responded with a bounce in her voice. "Just got back the other day, actually. I was in Europe for about ten days."

"Bet it wasn't a vacation."

"I did see some sights, but you know me, D. There's a lot to do."

"How's the boyfriend?"

"He's made me a big welcome-home feast. You should come up here and take some lessons from him. A man who cooks is a valuable commodity, D. It would really up your game."

"I have survived on oatmeal, protein shakes, and takeout for decades," he said. "It's a winning formula."

Serene laughed. "If you say so."

"You know about the accusations against Walter Gibbs?"

"Oh, I didn't miss that. You guys are still in business, aren't you?"

"He's been advising me on my deals since I got into artist management. But he's been a friend for years. You know, since the days of the bap and the boom."

"So you wanna know if he's on my list?"

D heard the tease in her voice and tried not to get angry. "I read all the stuff in the papers. I talked to him. But I trust you and your sources more than newspapers—and even more than him, I guess."

"Let's put it this way—he is not a priority for me," Serene said smoothly. "These days, I focus on traffickers. Big, bad, stinking fish. But if I were still interested in record-business people like Dr. Funk, I'm sure I would have encountered Gibbs."

"So you believe it's all true?"

"I can't speak to the truth of every accuser," Serene said. "I'm very aware that not every woman who wears a red hood really saw a wolf. But he was flagrant in using his power to abuse women psychologically, if not physically. These days, thankfully, there's a price to pay. When I started doing this work a few years ago, powerful men got away with whatever they wanted. Not so right now. So if you're calling for absolution for Walter Gibbs, you called the wrong woman."

"I wasn't," D said. "Or maybe I was a little. I know your heart and your commitment. So I believe you. With other people, I can try to punch holes in what they say. I know if I punch you, I'm gonna get hit back."

They both laughed at that truth.

"Listen," she said, "I hear the hurt in your voice. But it's not your burden, D."

"Well I'm not sure about that, but I do have something else I feel guilty about, and *this* I had a direct impact on."

"What am I, your priest?"

"No, though you do look good in black," he said. "I wanna hire you to go down to Atlanta and check on a woman for me."

"I just got back from Europe, D. Unlike you, I have a love life."

"Let me just kick the ballistics and see what you think."

CHAPTER NINETEEN

BAD AND BOUJEE

Two black men sat in a black Cadillac ATS Sedan under a streetlight in College Park, Georgia, an 80 percent African American town just beyond the Atlanta city limits. From outside the car, the men's faces were obscured by waves of smoke and weirdly illuminated by the red flames on the tips of their respective blunts (they weren't the types to share) and the glow of the dashboard radio. A Migos Spotify playlist was pumping. If Rasheeda Jackson had looked their way while exiting the East Point MARTA rail station, she might have thought the two men were wearing shifting reddish-green masks.

But Rasheeda didn't look because her eyes and ears were filled with content from her phone—music from 2 Chainz and a Snapchat makeup tutorial from her girlfriend Kandi. Rasheeda didn't really need the help—she was flawless, from her glowing bronze cheeks to her tapered eyebrows—but it never hurt to clock the competition.

When the Caddy pulled up next to her as she walked along East Main Street, Rasheeda didn't blink, slow down, or stumble. Men had been hollering at her from cars since she was twelve. She'd been embarrassed by the attention at thirteen, flattered by it at fifteen, and now, newly seventeen (though her fake ID said twenty-one), it was just boring. So Rasheeda wasn't even paying attention when a man hopped out of the passenger side and came toward her with his big hands outstretched. By the time Rasheeda felt his presence, he was standing a foot away.

"Boo!" said Gucci G.

Rasheeda jumped and then hit the man with a playful smack on his broad chest. "Gucci, you shouldn't play like that."

"Scared yo ass, huh?" he said through his gold fronts. "I know you down to make some money, sis."

"So you here waitin' on me? I must be something special."

"You out here fishin' for a compliment, huh? What you want me to say? We wouldn't be here if you weren't lit. Now, you want this money or not?"

Rasheeda smiled coyly and then joined Gucci G and Devon in the Caddy sedan and drove off.

Serene Powers swung her Audi out of its parking space and followed the trio into Atlanta's world of sex for sale.

Serene had been on Gucci G for two days, watching him pick up girls and transport clients from hotels, motels, and the airport. But so far she hadn't found a link to Dorita or a connection to Lil Daye. Dorita's coworkers at Verizon hadn't heard from her since she e-mailed in her resignation. Her mother told folks that Dorita had gone on vacation to Florida with a "boyfriend," though she actually hadn't heard from her in two weeks.

Serene was wearing black Lululemon yoga pants, black boots, a black Raiders hoodie, a black baseball cap, and dark-green shades. On the seat next to her was a black backpack full of lethal items.

When the Caddy stopped at a town house in the Atlanta suburb of John's Creek, Rasheeda and Gucci G got out the car but didn't head to the front door, instead going around the side of the large house. Serene followed them with the zoom function on her iPhone. Gucci G soon came back to the Caddy, which then drove off. This was the place; Serene was sure of it. She turned off the tracker she'd placed on Gucci G's ride, pulled out her laptop, and typed in the address.

With some searching around, Serene found the floor plan for the house and then checked the time: in twenty minutes it would be dark.

A Toyota Camry pulled up in front of the house. A skinny white man who spent too much time bent over at his job walked up to the front door and pressed the buzzer. After some conversation through the intercom, the door opened and a woman—fifties, short, and light-skinned—stuck her hand out and asked for ID. After looking it and him over, the woman let him in and then glanced left and right before closing the door.

A few minutes later, a baby-blue BMX pulled up in front of the house, depositing a short Asian man in a dark suit and glasses, who gazed at his phone before pressing the front-door buzzer and engaging with the same woman.

It was the third visitor who really got Serene's attention. A red-and-white Escalade pulled up and parked in the driveway. A large balding black man walked up to the front door smoking a cigar and wearing a Lil Daye T-shirt. He tapped his phone, the door opened, and he entered.

According to the photos D had forwarded to Serene, this was Antonie Newton Davis, a.k.a. Ant, Lil Daye's business partner and, based on information from her anti–human trafficking contacts, an investor in various sex-based enterprises in ATL. People said he'd been a pimp, but Ant had never been arrested for it, or if he had, it was when he'd been underage so the records were sealed. What wasn't clear was whether the sex trade had given him the earnings to support Lil Daye's career, or if it was his music money that had allowed him to dabble in the sex trade. But ultimately those niceties didn't matter to Serene.

If Ant was making money off the exploitation of women, he was a villain.

Serene saw that there were bars on the ground-floor windows, but the second-floor windows just had reinforced glass. There were security cameras by the front and back doors, but none on the upstairs windows. She figured they'd have silent alarms on the windows, but not linked to a security company. She doubted any of the folks at this brothel could really fight. Probably one or two big, slow guys like Ant. There would be guns; it was Atlanta. However, would they risk the sound of gunfire? If they were stupid they would, and likely they were stupid. The key would be to find Dorita quickly (if she was inside). Everything would flow from that. The longer Serene was in there, the riskier it would be.

She moved to the side of the house, climbed up on the ledge to a first-floor window, reached up to hook ropes around the bars, and then pulled herself up so that she could see into a second-floor bedroom. No one was in there.

There were absolutely smarter and quieter ways to go about entry, but Serene's patience had worn out. She placed a tiny explosive device on the glass, swung her body below the window, and clicked an app on her phone. The glass blew. Thirty seconds later, Serene was in the second-floor bedroom. She listened. Lumbering feet on the stairs. She got low by the side door as the doorknob turned. The door flung open. A big man stormed in. His breath stopped when Serene's foot slammed into his sternum. His arms flew up; his legs buckled. His clothes smelled of takeout Chinese. He clutched his heart. His breath smelled nasty. Serene scooped up the Beretta on the floor and shoved it into her jacket.

She descended the staircase one slow step at a time.

"Dougie," the madam called, "are you okay?"

"No, Dougie isn't okay. He needs a doctor!" She could see the madam holding a .22 with her eyes shifting from the staircase to the back door.

"I'll shoot!" the woman said.

"I have Dougie's gun and a bulletproof vest on," Serene replied. "If you wanna do it, we can do it, but it's your life."

A door slammed as the madam, who had *Anji* tattooed on her right arm, considered her next move. Ant's car could be heard pulling out of the driveway.

"Your boss is gone," Serene said.

"He ain't my boss!" Anji shouted.

"He waited till I kicked Dougie's ass before he ran. Only a boss would have left you in danger."

"He's gonna call people. You need to leave."

"I intend to. I just wanna show you a photo. I'm looking for a girl."

Anti snorted. "You could have just buzzed," she said.

"I'm coming down the steps. You don't shoot at me, I won't kill you."

Serene extended the photo out toward Anji's face. When the madam stuck her neck out a little to look at it, Serene swung her left leg around, knocking Anji and her gun to the floor. Serene scooped up the weapon and then jumped on the madam, pinning her arms to the floor.

"You know the safety was still on?"

"Fuck you, bitch!" the woman spat.

"I'm gonna show you this picture and please don't lie. As you see, I'll hit a woman as quickly as I'll hit a man."

From down the hall a voice yelled, "What's going on, Anji?!"

Serene pushed both her knees into the madam's elbows. "Tell them to come out, Anji."

Reluctantly, Anji did as she was told. Following the opening and closing of doors, there was fumbling of clothes and then embarrassed male faces as they escaped the house. Anji, Rasheeda, and two other young black women named Sales and Dymond stood in the living room. Each looked at the photo of Dorita, but only Rasheeda flashed recognition in her eyes.

"So you know her?" Serene asked.

"I never said that," Rasheeda snapped.

"Don't say shit." This was Anji. Serene reached over and backhanded the madam with her gun. The woman dropped to the floor, clutched her cheek, and moaned.

"So," Serene said, "when's the last time you saw Dorita?"

Rasheeda was having a hard time focusing as her gaze locked on the fallen Anji.

"Don't look at her. Look at me."

"Two weeks ago. At a party."

"Was she with Lil Daye?"

"No."

"Was Ant there?"

Rasheeda evidently decided this was too much cooperation and said, "Who?"

Bad decision. Serene punched her in the stomach. The young woman keeled over in pain.

"Okay, catch your breath. I don't wanna have to do that again. But—"

"Yeah, she was with Ant," Rasheeda said. "But that's all I know."

"No Lil Daye, right?"

"No."

"Shut up, bitch!" Anji barked from the floor.

Serene walked over and kicked her right between her breasts. The lady pimp's groans filled the room.

"Okay, ladies," Serene said, "who wants to go with me? I figure working conditions here just got much worse." The three young women traded looks but none of them moved. "Your call."

Serene walked out the front door and, to her surprise, spied an Atlanta PD patrol car turning onto the block. One of the neighbors must have called about the exploding window. The patrol car stopped at a house down the block as Serene got in her car.

She wasn't sure if the police had seen her so Serene didn't start her engine. The two patrolmen—a white male and a black female—walked up the block and, using flashlights, spotted broken glass outside the brothel. Things got more interesting when two cars roared onto the block and pulled into the brothel's driveway. With guns drawn, Ant and three beefy cronies dashed onto the front lawn. The two police officers pulled their weapons. A shouting match ensued between the law and Ant. Soon, Anji stuck her head out the door and began yelling too.

Serene wished she could stay, but the timing was perfect to get the hell away.

CHAPTER TWENTY

THAT'S WHAT I LIKE

Din Tai Fung, a chain of exceptional dumpling spots, was dipping its toe in the Los Angeles market after many successful years in Taiwan. D had eaten at its flagship restaurant in Shanghai and had been knocked out by its tasty prawn, veggie, and pork specialties. When he'd discovered there was one located in an Arcadia strip mall, he'd made several pilgrimages out to that largely Chinese area of the Valley and was not disappointed.

When D found out that Kurtz's office was located in Century City, he was overjoyed. Din Tai Fung had just taken over a large space in the renovated Westfield Mall, literally one long block away from the area's twin towers. He didn't know what Kurtz wanted or if there was really a deal to be made, but he was damn sure he was getting his dumpling game on. After a couple of plates of dumplings, any deal would just be the spicy sauce on his meal.

D brought along Marcy Mui, the young Chinese-Korean woman who was working as his assistant while developing her own management portfolio under D Management's banner. She'd been recommended by Sun Hee Pak, a big K-Town businesswoman whose daughter, Michelle, D had loved and lost. But Mrs. Pak, never one to toss away a potential biz partner or client, remained cordial with D. So when he needed someone to go with Night on his early trips to Korea, Mrs. Pak recommended Marcy to him. Marcy had an undergrad degree in business administration, was planning to attend USC's law school, and was working as D's liaison with the Korean music business for his deals involving Night.

"I read Kurtz's profile in *Forbes*," Marcy said to D as they got ready to head over.

"And?"

"Seems to be moderate on every issue. He's donated to both Dems and Republicans. For a big corporate dude, he's surprisingly neutral politically."

"You seem skeptical," D said.

"Nobody with that much money lacks a political agenda. Not these days."

"Do you have a problem with me meeting with him?"

"Not at all," Marcy said. "If his proposition is beneficial for our client, then I support it. If this deal turns into something *really* good, maybe we can get him to donate to prison reform, gun control, and other issues important to Lil Daye's fans."

"Fine," D said. "But let's not get into that until we get this paper."

Diversified International Brands had three floors in one of the Century Plaza Towers, a mini version of the late World Trade Center in New York. A perky brunette assistant named Ingrid guided them through smoky-glass doors down a long wood-paneled corridor lined with black-and-white photos of American West landscapes. D thought they might have been Ansel Adams pics but decided not to ask. He'd suddenly grown nervous and decided to save his limited introductory chitchat for the meeting with Kurtz.

Kurtz was in his late fifties and tanned, with gray hair, small eyes, and a lipless mouth. He was stocky, with the chest and arms of an avid weightlifter. With his blue-and-white-striped shirt, navy-blue pants, and black slip-on loafers, Kurtz carried a casual-Friday aura, though this was Wednesday. He didn't dumb himself down because he was meeting with a black man, but he wasn't giving off full-court, master-of-the-universe attitude.

"So, Mr. Hunter, it is a pleasure to meet you," he said with a professional smile.

"Great to meet you as well, Mr. Kurtz. It's an understatement to say I've heard a lot about you."

"Ditto on this end. Any man who irritates Amos Pilgrim and manages to stay in business is a man worth knowing."

"Where did you hear that about Amos and me? I know *he* didn't tell you that."

Kurtz chuckled. "I asked him 'cause Amos knows everybody."

"What did he say?"

"His tone told me everything I needed, even when he complimented you. But no worries: we were destined to meet. After all, we're already in business together."

"How's that?"

"I own a piece of the hologram company, Future Life," Kurtz said, clearly pleased with himself. "Which you wisely got your clients involved with. Your artists have certainly been adding value to that venture."

D was surprised. "R'Kaydia never mentioned that you were a backer."

"It's not something we trumpet in the media, and to be blunt, it's not yet profitable for us. It took a long time to build the technology, and holograms as a form of purchased entertainment haven't been as widely accepted as we'd hoped. But the thing with entertainment plays is you never know how folks in the real world will use them. You may plan X and they use it for Y. The upside is you make unexpected relationships. So, like I said, we are already helping each other." Kurtz nodded to his assistant and a video screen in his office flashed on. "Before you speak with your client, I want to show you something."

Lil Daye's "Hy Life" burst out of two speakers and the word SINSERE in black Gothic lettering against a red background popped on the screen. That was followed by images from Lil Daye's life and videos, intercut with shots of strip clubs, luxury cars, slim and thick women in slinky dresses, and lots of equally curvy gold-and-white bottles with SINSERE written on the label. The last image was SINSERE and then underneath, THE CÎROC OF THE SOUTH.

"Whoa," said D. "That's amazing."

"What do you think, young lady?" Kurtz asked Marcy.

"How does Sinsere taste?"

Kurtz laughed. "That's a great question."

While his assistant went to get D and Marcy a sample, Kurtz pitched: "We've monitored what the Sean Combs/Cîroc relationship has accomplished and we believe a connection between Lil Daye and our Sinsere vodka will dwarf it. We'll learn from their mistakes and do what worked better than they did. This deal would be a long relationship.

"When hip hop first caught on I was appalled," Kurtz went on. "Honestly, it was too loud, ghetto, and seemed dangerous for the country. Then when Run-D.M.C. made that deal with Adidas, I realized what rap was: a delivery system, an advertising medium. It put ideas, attitudes, and products into the consciousness of listeners. Unlike advertising, which can lead to resistance and tuning out, rap was readily accepted. Rappers were natural endorsers and spokespeople."

Clearly Kurtz wasn't a hip hop fan, but his clinical analysis meant dude took the culture seriously and, unlike many older men of his generation, had turned disdain into dollars. Kurtz had no problem putting cash in the bank accounts of black people (as long as his bag was bigger). D didn't *like* Kurtz—there was definitely a block of ice behind those blue eyes—but there was nothing wrong with a cold-blooded businessman if you were on the same side of the deal.

Every now and then, Kurtz cast an appraising gaze on Marcy's legs peeking out from under her yellow sundress. His demeanor was professional, but D glimpsed the inner man. The assistant came back with a tray of three glasses of golden-brown fluid. Not only did it look as thick as syrup, but it tasted like sweet cherry cough medicine with a strong alcohol kick.

Looking closely at D's and Marcy's faces, Kurtz said, "Our market research indicated that this taste and texture was right for Sinsere." He could tell they didn't like it. But then again, all of them knew that no one in that room was Sinsere's target market. "I want to send a case to your client and then close this deal."

D agreed and they all shook hands.

On the way out of the building, Marcy said with her best hip hop accent, "D, that was like sippin' on some sizzurp."

D replied, "Well, I gotta a feeling Lil Daye and his team are gonna love it. Especially after DIB puts several million guaranteed dollars on the table."

"That Kurtz gave me creeps," she said. "I wanna dig into him some more."

"Do that on your time," D said. "This deal is worth a lot to our client, to this company, and to you—come bonus time."

CHAPTER TWENTY-ONE
BLEEDING LOVE

Dorita wasn't sure if she should go. Ant had never said much to her before. But he was Lil Daye's business partner so it made sense that he'd handle things. Dorita had hoped she'd be dealing with that manager from Los Angeles—keeping things professional. Yet Ant was in ATL and they did know each other, so despite her misgivings, she was going to show up.

It was only fair. It really was. She'd kept quiet and played her position. She knew Lil Daye was married when they started hooking up. He'd never lied and she was no fool. But when Dorita heard that he was shooting a family reality show starring his bitch of a wife, it was too much. It hurt her, especially after having learned way too much about Mama's ways.

Lil Daye wouldn't support Dorita's goals. She wanted to be a producer. She didn't want the light. She wanted to be the flame that *made* the light. Her beats were lit. Everybody told her that. Even Ant knew that. She just wanted to be part of his production team, then find her own artists. But Lil Daye always shut that down. She was more than a sidepiece and he knew it. So she grew tired of waiting. This money would help Dorita upgrade her equipment.

Dorita took a selfie. She was wearing black stretch pants, a jean jacket, a black Travis Scott tee, and Gucci shades. She wanted to document this day, the day she moved on from Lil Daye and transitioned into the next phase of her life. She didn't see what she was doing as blackmail in any way. This was just a long-overdue investment, an investment by Lil Daye in her talents, not some payment for sucking his okay dick. But now he was going to have to do the right thing, and that's what was important.

With that thought in mind, Dorita left her apartment.

Serene downloaded the file and peered at it with sad, heavy eyes. It was from the United Nations Office on Drugs and Crime and contained two attachments. The first was a map of sex-trafficking patterns from Africa, Asia, and Eastern Europe. All the routes depicted involved mobsters, trial leaders, terrorist cells, and other undercover agents of capitalism who profited from the selling of bodies in the modern slave trade, in particular the sale of women (and some men) for the pleasure of men. Moreover, most of the shipping lines of human cargo led to Europe. Despite the racism, xenophobia, and Islamophobia, this illustrated the fact that men wanted to have sex with poorer people from around the globe.

The other document was titled "2016 UNODC Global Report on Trafficking in Persons" and was a summary of activity around the world. Serene went to the United States section where chief destinations for trafficked people were Los Angeles, New York, Chicago, and Atlanta. Serene sat back in her chair and reflected on all the rooms she'd been in and the people this report was based on.

She'd been working almost full-time on sex trafficking for several years, all the ugliness she'd encountered weighing her down like barbells on her chest.

Progress had been fleeting. Some bad people in jail. Some girls returned home. Some networks damaged. A lot of "some." But the flood of bodies, the cold current of hateful desire, and the commodification of intimacy were unstoppable forces. Every day, it seemed, Serene received more confirmation that people were shit.

She wasn't Superwoman, Wonder Woman, or Batwoman. She was just a person who wanted to help one girl (a girl she never found) and then dove into the sewer, feeling pure in her convictions. Now her hair, her body, and her spirit were covered in human stink. Everyone she'd punched, every door she'd smashed, and every corrupt official she'd disrespected were reasons to hate being alive. Sharing air with these people disgusted her. She'd come to know that not far beneath the rules of civilization was a beastly creed of brutality, sometimes muted, but always there, like the low chants of ancient priests. She closed her computer screen and her eyes, but there was no unseeing, and no forgetting.

CHAPTER TWENTY-TWO

I GET THE BAG

Since moving to Los Angeles, D had identified three distinct entrepreneurial hustles in the City of Angels: some hustled their minds, a bunch hustled their bodies, and a host of folks hustled their spirit. These hustles existed all over the world, but LA had its particular spin.

The TV and film biz—writers, directors, producers, agents—was filled with mind hustlers who either created IPs (a.k.a. intellectual properties), rebooted IPs, purchased IPs, or highjacked IPs for fun and profit. Whether they were nerds or hacks, Ivy League or community college grads, the LA mind hustle was on display in coffee shops and on Soho House sofas.

The body hustle in LA encompassed trainers and instructors of every conceivable physical specialty: pole dancing, boxing, surfing, booty tightening, hamstring stretching, cryo freezing with abs the furious focus—at every gym and studio. Flat was not enough. The goal was a six-pack, eight-pack, and angles of definition not previously seen in nature.

Pilates and yoga instructors were as common in LA as traffic jams. These same people were also dancers, actors, and models. Video-game fit and Pirelli-calendar fine. Perhaps because D was jaded, he found much of this physical perfection stunningly uniform, like glancing rapidly through his Instagram "Videos to Watch" feed. All of them were united by their combination of tan skin, enhanced lips, moussed hair, bare midriffs, ripped jeans, athletic sleeves, Alo yoga pants, extended eyelashes, and excessive flexing.

Of this get-money trio, D's favorite were the spirit hustlers, who were attached to the mind hustle through meditation and the body hustle through yoga. "Wellness," a word he'd never heard before going west, was their trendy branding umbrella. He'd met so many folks—most of them women—who led group meditation, were self-described shamans (shawomen?), sold crystals, advised via online classes, read tarot cards, practiced Hinduism, Taoism, Buddhism, and in general offered themselves as pathways to transcendence.

D was thinking about LA hustle as he sat in Viacom's lobby waiting on Leigh Amber Daye, a.k.a. Mama Daye, to arrive for their VH1 meeting. He'd once been squarely in the realm of the body hustle as a big black man who kept people safe. Now he was a mind hustler, learning the ropes of pitching shows and scripts. Something told him that the spirit hustle was in his future, though he had no idea how he'd make that leap.

Mama Daye arrived loud as a boom box at a silent meditation. "Hello, you big, beautiful black man!" She walked up to D with a big smile and wide-opens arms. Way in the background, standing by a Rolls Royce with his arms folded, was Ant. Apparently he'd survived his confrontation with the APD.

Serene had not found out much else about Dorita in Atlanta. The tip about Florida had gone nowhere. Lots of women were missing down there and lots of names had been changed. Some women stripped, some did webcams or worked for escort services.

Serene told D that maybe Ant had dragged Dorita into that work—if she was still alive. Serene had checked out the morgue and found a few women who matched Dorita's description, but thankfully none were the missing woman. Undoubtedly Ant had been involved in her disappearance, likely at Lil Daye's instigation. What D hadn't decided yet was what he should do with that information.

Mama Daye's long, shiny Remy weave was whatever color suited her that week (burgundy today). Her cocoa skin was augmented by bold eye shadow, lipstick, and foundation choices. For the meeting, she was wearing a black-and-white Ivy Park ensemble. The top was a touch baggy, but the tight white pants illuminated her ample hips. D nearly blushed when he looked at her because Mama Daye's gynecological information was overheating his manhood, not a condition he wanted to experience in the presence of a client's wife.

D asked, "Is Ant coming in with us?"

"Nawn, he's gonna stay with the car," Mama Daye said. "Acts like he owns it. He knows you got this anyway. C'mon, honey, let's go get this bag."

Ten minutes later, Mama and D were sitting in a Viacom office and she was running the room.

"It was *lit*," she told the collected executives, referencing a party Oprah had hosted the previous weekend. D glanced over at the men and women and smiled. This deal was done the minute Mama Daye entered the conference room. The fact that she had 5.3 million followers on Twitter and six million subscribers on YouTube for her makeup tips and life advice spoke for itself.

D then took the whole meeting to another level when he guaranteed that DIB, including the soon-to-launch Sinsere, would help sponsor the show and provide digital assets to expand its reach. VH1, BET, and MTV would all air the show, making Mama Daye a Viacom ambassador, with the plot of Season One leading to the making of her first single, which would of course be titled "Mama's Daye" and be released on Mother's Day.

Mama was giddy when they left the meeting. "Lil said you were sharp," she said, "but them motherfuckers in there weren't ready."

As his client luxuriated in her dreams of Cardi B–like success, D steeled himself for a serious conversation with Ant. The bald, bulky man now sat on a bench outside the Viacom building sipping on a frosty Starbucks treat and messing around on his phone.

"They want me," Mama Daye announced.

"Not surprised, Ma," Ant said. "We got a big bag coming, D?"

"Real big."

"Way to do your job," the bald man said with feigned enthusiasm.

They'd never be close friends, but D had expected a little more love from Ant. *Jealous hearts are always cold*, he thought, and then walked his Atlanta associates to the parking area. D wasn't going to get into the whole Dorita thing with Mama Daye there. In any event, she was heading back to Atlanta to be with the kids. The next night, Ant, Lil Daye, and D were having a private dinner with Kurtz. It would be a long ride out to Malibu.

CHAPTER TWENTY-THREE

MOTORSPORT

"**H**ow much farther is it?" Lil Daye asked.

"I'm not sure," Ant said. "GPS says ten minutes."

The Benz rolled north on the Pacific Coast Highway with BlocBoy JB & Drake's "Look Alive" filling the air along with the scent of a hybrid THC flowing from the cigarette between Lil Daye's lips. Ant was driving and D was in the backseat next to Lil Daye. They'd been invited up to Kurtz's beach house for a small celebration of their new business relationship.

Though he would never say it out loud, Lil Daye was happy his wife couldn't make it (and that Kurtz couldn't reschedule to accommodate her), because he'd been told Kurtz's LA parties could turn salacious. Whether or not the cultural developments of the last few years had changed Kurtz's swag, the trio didn't know, but Lil Daye had his fingers crossed, hoping he hadn't missed all the fun he'd heard about.

But before they reached the dinner, it was time for D to ask some questions. "Yo, Ant," he said conversationally, "I read online you almost had a shoot-out with the Atlanta cops."

"Shit," Ant said, "that wasn't a real thing. Some cops stopped my car and started talking shit. You know how they be treating us down there, right, Daye?"

"Oh yeah," the MC agreed. "They know our cars and plates. They just fuck with us 'cause they ain't us."

"Yeah," D said, "no doubt. I've had my run-ins with the police over the years. It's just the kind of thing that the white folks in the branding business might get a little worried about."

"Long as it wasn't me," Lil Daye said, "we'll be all right, D. I understand what ya sayin'. Ant got a low profile though."

From the front Ant asked sharply, "What website you see it on?"

"It was on Twitter somewhere," D said, lying casually. "I should've screenshot it."

"Hmm," Ant said, "I'm surprised no one forwarded it to me."

D wanted to ask about Dorita, but coming behind the cagey way his two Atlanta partners were downplaying the police incident, he'd wait awhile. Linking the two would give away that he knew a lot more than he was saying.

Kurtz's glass-and-chrome home was on a cliff overlooking the Pacific, like Tony Stark's in *Iron Man*. The white walls were decorated with large abstract canvases by well-known eighties painters. The furniture was so shiny the leather couches reflected light. There was nothing warm or womanly about Kurtz's Malibu spot, though his company's website touted a twenty-year marriage to his childhood sweetheart.

The dinner of some twenty or so folks was peppered with women of color in their late twenties and early thirties—black, brown, yellow, and all shades in between—wearing tremendously high heels. Except for Lil Daye, Ant, and D, all the men were either white or Asian, dressed casually but tastefully, with lots of expensive watches. Kurtz worked the room, filling glasses with champagne and giving Lil Daye insights into why investing in art was the next move for the MC's money. Ant hung on his every word; D had never seen this side of Ant—he looked like a child happy about after-school tutoring.

"D Hunter?"

He turned to see a willowy, tattooed, natural-haired brunette standing next to his chair. "My name is Maggie LeClair," she said. "I'm friends with Ray Ray. He speaks so highly of you, I wanted to introduce myself. Can I sit down?"

A chair was found and Maggie, who surveyed D with warmth and apparent amusement, chatted him up. As artfully arranged plates of kale salad, seafood, and several vegan entrées arrived, Maggie charmed D with tales of coming to LA from NOLA to model and dance in music videos. D had met many lovely, ambitious women since relocating west, but Maggie had a light, earthy quality different from the metallic sheen so many Hollywood women developed as armor.

She really got D's ear when she started talking about Kurtz. "This is my third time here," she said, "but I have friends who've been coming here for parties and such for several years."

"Is the wife ever here?"

"You ever see that old TV detective show *Columbo*? My daddy still watches it on cable and they never show the wife. Whenever my mother is late—which is all the time—my daddy calls her Mrs. Columbo 'cause she ain't there. Same goes for Mrs. Kurtz—she ain't here."

D glanced up to see Lil Daye smoking a joint by the window with two women who looked like models, looking out at the Pacific. Ant was now in Kurtz's ear and the industrialist was listening with interest.

"I assume Kurtz has made a move on you?"

"Is the ocean water?" she said, laughing. "But I don't get down like that. He's married and I am not about to become some rich man's mistress. He keeps inviting me out here though. The food is good, the view's amazing, and I meet cool people."

"Thank you," D said. "I'm flattered."

"You're welcome." Maggie then lowered her voice. "Plus, that very straight-looking man is into some freaky shit. Literally."

"Excuse me?"

She laughed again, a deep husky sound that made D smile.

"Let's take a tour of the place," she said. "He'll think we went to fuck. It'll be a good look for you."

D could feel Kurtz's hot, uncomfortable gaze on them as they strolled out of the dining room up a flight of stairs. The second floor was lined with bedrooms, each lit by blue, green, or red lights. At the end of the hall was a master bedroom. "You know your way around here, don't you?"

"Knowledge is king, right?"

Instead of comforting D, this made him wonder if Maggie was about to set him up. His body tensed as they entered the room. Maybe being alone with this woman wasn't a good idea.

Inside a high-ceilinged, blue-lit bedroom were a stunning view of the ocean, a huge Basquiat painting, and a king-size bed with a plexiglass structure about six feet above it. Next to the plexiglass was a clear plastic ladder.

"What the fuck?"

Maggie chuckled. "Thought you'd seen everything, huh?"

"Okay." D was totally confused. He glanced at the bed and then at Maggie. "What the hell is this for?"

"Lie on the bed."

"I'm not lying in this guy's bed."

"Don't be afraid, big man. I got you." She guided a very reluctant D to the bed and pushed him down. He looked up at the clear plexiglass and through to the ceiling. Maggie walked over to the ladder, scooted it closer to the plexiglass, and climbed up. From the bed D saw some very expensive underwear between Maggie's spread legs.

"He gets a peep show?"

She giggled. "He gets a shit-and-piss show."

"Stop!" D hopped out of the bed. "You are fucking kidding me."

Maggie was laughing so hard she could barely make it back down the ladder. "I guess Mrs. Kurtz wasn't down anymore. So now she farms out the work."

"Have you done this for Kurtz?"

"I keep my shit to myself," Maggie said, and laughed some more. D was amused and disgusted. "But I have girlfriends who aren't so shy. Plenty of sports cars rolling around this town have been financed by this shitstorm. You hungry, D?"

"Stop it. But I think I'll have a drink or a joint or something."

Back downstairs, the boater-hatted DJ Cassidy appeared and set up his turntables. The dining tables had been pushed back. Dancing soon commenced. Lil Daye seemed a bit jealous that D had bonded with Maggie, trying to kick it to her at one point, but she stayed close to D the rest of the night and into the morning. At one point, Kurtz pulled D to the side. Not to talk business but to say, "That Maggie is a stunner. You did well tonight."

"To be honest, I didn't do much."

"That's always best," Kurtz said. "If you're working too hard, it's probably not for you. I like you and your partners, D. Lil Daye is the star. Ant is the street. You have presence. People are attracted to how solid you are. Hold onto that. Integrity is as valuable as a diamond."

D went out in the morning chill, watching the dawn break over the beach. He felt a presence and turned to the side, and there was Maggie, barefoot, with a blanket over her shoulders. "Your friends just left with some of my friends," she said. "You need a ride? I live in Echo Park but I can drive you if you'd like."

D nodded off on the way home, waking up as they reached the farmers market on Fairfax and 3rd. "I'm hungry," he said.

"Okay," Maggie replied, "it'll cost you."

They sat there in their party clothes, eating croissants and drinking tea as workers set up stalls and swept up yesterday's trash. D asked, "You googled me before the party?"

"I did," she admitted with a smile. "You sounded like you'd be the most interesting person there."

"I'm afraid to ask if I lived up to the online hype."

"Then don't."

They both laughed. D hadn't enjoyed anyone's company this much in a quite a while. Maggie had a sparkle to her. She also knew things D didn't, which he found very attractive.

"I think we'll be friends," he said.

"We'll see," she said, smiling as she sipped her tea. "We'll see."

CHAPTER TWENTY-FOUR
SURE THING

Maggie LeClair loved her jab. Her hook was good and up-percuts strong, but her jab snapped like a serpent's tongue. Her father, a day laborer in New Orleans, had taught her the basics one afternoon when he hadn't fallen asleep as soon as he got home. Her daddy told her, "You jab a fool in the nose or eye or mouth and that'll stop most of them cold. After that you can do anything you want—run, kick 'em, trip 'em, bite 'em. Most women will just grab the part you hit and worry about their looks. Most men—well, a lot of men—will be so shocked they got hit so hard by a woman that they'll take a step back. So then you can decide whether to fight or run. But that jab—that jab will give you the time to decide."

From that day on, Maggie shadowboxed, watched Daddy's old Ali DVDs, and eventually began slipping into a gym in Tremé for sparring sessions. Rumble on Sunset Boulevard here in LA was far from that ratty NOLA gym. This high-tech cardio spot was as much club as gym, sporting hip hop tracks, bright instructional signage (#1 was jab, #2 was cross, etc.), and hyped-up, superfit trainers and life coaches.

She'd traveled from LA (Louisiana) to LA (Hollywood). Back home, she was a skinny tomboy with overly long limbs. Maggie was a multihyphenate in a city powered by talented dreamers. She glanced in the mirrors that fronted the room and surveyed the truly fit, the strivers, and the merely enthusiastic all swinging gloves at new water-based heavy bags.

After class Maggie took an Instagram photo with her class instructor, a self-described warrior princess named Lelia, and then walked out onto Sunset Boulevard heading west. Posted up at the corner was the same homeless man she'd seen on the Strip the past couple of months. He was tall, black, in his forties, always wearing a dirty overcoat draped over his ragged clothes and shoes. He was talking rapidly today but Maggie couldn't make out the words.

The homeless issue in LA really troubled her. Even at the lowest point of post-Katrina NOLA, she'd never seen the displacement and mental illness she'd witnessed in this city. She'd been volunteering downtown at a food pantry every few weeks. That area may have been the historical home of homelessness in the city, but there were encampments and tent cities as far west as the border of Beverly Hills, and then scores of lost people in Santa Monica.

To Maggie, the homeless were like ghosts in the machine, ever present but never acknowledged, at least not by the wannabe fab people she rolled with. It didn't make Maggie feel guilty—she'd only been in LA a few years, so she didn't own the problem. Still, she felt connected to them. Miss a couple of checks and your life was wrecked. She wanted to offer this man some money, but he was too far inside his head to be a beggar. She wondered how he ate and where he slept, but he didn't seem like someone you could get answers from.

Reaching the Sunset Plaza parking lot, Maggie made a left and then another left to a Chinese massage parlor, where she got the hour treatment with twenty additional minutes for a foot massage. There were audition pages to read and acting class to prepare for, but a little pampering never hurt anyone.

On the table, her mind drifted. Ballet class as kid. Volleyball games as a teen. Premed exams. Premed boredom. Football-player boyfriend. Mistake of a stupid weekend in Miami with an Instagram flirtation. Moving to LA along with her college BFF Leslie. Falling out with Leslie over a pair of borrowed boots. Living in a couple of places in the Valley before settling in North Hollywood.

Booking Wendy's and Kit Kat commercials back-to-back gave her the first taste of financial security in her young professional life. Being introduced to Samuel Kurtz at an art gallery opening on La Brea. Falling in with a squad of young women who attended his fabulous soirees in Malibu. Affirming that her power in Kurtz's world was in *not* sleeping with any of these rich dudes, despite the offers of jewelry and sports cars. And then there was the image of D Hunter.

Unlike most of the successful men she'd met in LA, D didn't present himself as a finished product. He was a man in transition, going from where he'd been to somewhere he wasn't sure of. There was space there for a woman. He wasn't prepared to fit you in as a trophy wife or to "sponsor" you. With D, Maggie suspected, you could create your own world in tandem with his and not just be pretty piece of his larger puzzle. Plus he was big, strong, cute, and vulnerable. There was a damaged child inside D Hunter, which gave him an air of intrigue.

After the massage, Maggie got back in her Prius and returned to her current reality. Bills due. Agents to call. Clothes to wash. The future wouldn't take care of itself. You had to be proactive and make a plan. She turned on Melanie Drift's podcast *Healing Is Not Linear,* which was a staple of her drives. Drift had become her guru as of late, a balm over all the little indignities of big-city life. Still, Maggie had to admit, as her car crawled across Sunset toward Crescent Heights, she really wished she could jab LA traffic right in its damn nose.

CHAPTER TWENTY-FIVE
THE DARKEST HEARTS

The Lodge Room was a converted Masonic temple in the once-gang-ridden, now hipster LA neighborhood of Highland Park, with a balcony that overlooked N. Figueroa Street next to a high-ceilinged bar/restaurant with an ornate chandelier and dinner booths along the walls.

In another room, there was a Masonic assembly hall turned performance space, with burnished dark-brown wood walls and the floor NBA-quality hardwood. The hall had a mysterious feel, as if the spirit of myriad Masonic rituals still hovered.

At the back of the room this night was a wide stage hosting something D hadn't seen in a while: a full old-school rhythm section, including an electric piano, augmented by four real string players, as dapper keyboardist Adrian Younge and former A Tribe Called Quest DJ Ali Shaheed Muhammad led their band, the Midnight Hour. The proudly analog ensemble made moody, independently released funk albums and composed scores for film and TV, including the retro-seventies music for Netflix's *Luke Cage*. Seeing Ali strictly as a bass player and not behind the ones and twos supporting Q-Tip and Phife Dawg always tripped D out.

Even more pleasing than watching this glorious band was seeing it fronted by Night, who was doing a guest slot with them.

They'd already worked out a very midseventies Marvin Gaye–like arrangement of Night's neosoul classic "Black Sex." But as D walked toward the stage, the Midnight Hour played the intro to a song D hadn't heard yet.

D had expected Night to want to perform "White Men in Suits." Instead, he was launching into a different song, from his recent "woke" period. He was calling it "The Darkest Hearts." It wasn't as explicit as "White Men," but had a haunting quality like one of Sade's ballads circa *Love Deluxe*.

The sun don't shine where I've been,
It's just gray with a slight gust of wind, but I'm not lost;
I'm not afraid.
I will hold your hand and we'll walk away,
The exit is close by and the gates are unlocked.
In the distance is clear sky and we are no longer blocked.

I can see (into the darkest hearts), I lose me (in the darkest hearts),
I break free (from the darkest hearts).

A change is gonna come, I promise you that,
But we gotta walk till we run,
And I pick up my gat,
Then it's time for our fun.

I can see (into the darkest hearts), I lose me (in the darkest hearts),
I break free (from the darkest hearts), the darkest hearts,
Deep in the darkest hearts.

When the song was over Night looked down at his manager and said, "Work in progress, D."

"A good one, my dude."

"Yeah," Night said proudly. "A recent arrival."

In the long, narrow backstage area of the Lodge Room, Night and D sat on a lumpy green sofa, marveling at how good it was to hear live strings and a tight R&B/jazz band. "It must be sweet feeling that behind you," D said.

"Yes indeed." Night was as happy as D had seen him in a while. "That shit gives you life. Once I have that audience in front of me, who knows where that will take me."

"Looking forward to you turning it out."

D and Night shared much unspoken history. Back when D ran his New York nightclub security company, Night was an aspiring singer and part-time gigolo for high-post white ladies of a certain age. He had been "managed" by a very enterprising Italian woman named Rafaella, who found the clients and set the prices (though if they wanted to buy Night gifts, that was between him and the ladies). It didn't matter how old or wrinkled the client was, Night found a way to pleasure her.

Night used this illicit cash to cut demos, pay musicians, and hide his embarrassment behind plumes of marijuana. He'd been a downtown nightlife vampire, chatting up record executives and artsy fly girls with equal vigor. His life changed when he was at an Upper East Side gig involving masks of jazz icons. He'd argued with a woman wearing a strap-on dildo who wanted to fuck him. Night had left the party early. The next day, the woman who'd booked him was found dead and the male escort was the number one suspect.

Helping Night avoid a murder rap was the first time D had stepped out of his doorman role and into quasi-detective status. Through some physical force and using his nightlife contacts, D helped Night clear his name. But that wasn't the only time D came to Night's rescue.

While driving back from JFK Airport one night, the singer had been kidnapped by a motorcycle gang. It was D who delivered the ransom money and cracked the case.

These life-and-death situations had bonded these two men, though they rarely talked about them. For both, it was another life in another city. If D had his way, he'd just manage Night full-time. He loved Night's spirit despite how self-destructive the singer could be. But with the economics of entertainment these days, it didn't make sense. Living off 10 to 15 percent of a veteran black male R&B star's earnings was no way to survive in a marketplace where hip hop was pop and R&B vocalizing had been usurped by auto-tuned MCs in turtlenecks. In the newly woke Night, D saw potential for an important *What's Going On* or *Black Messiah* type album. But would anybody care? D wasn't sure.

"Yo," Night said, his tone changing, "you know a woman attorney named Belinda Bowman?"

"Met her once with Amos Pilgrim. Seems like she wants to get money. She want you as a client?"

"Yeah, D. Good-looking sista too."

"Indeed."

"But I'm not sure about her. She said she knew you. But then she went into a whole thing about how she could get me endorsements and I was like, *I have a manager*. Felt like she was overstepping."

D chuckled. "Its all good, Night. She's a wannabe baller. I'm guessing she was just tryin' to close."

D didn't feel threatened by Bowman. Hype and hustle fueled the entertainment business like drills did oil. It actually made him feel excited for Night. If a comer like Bowman saw value in his client, it meant there were deals to be made. *Let the sharks circle*, he thought. *I got my harpoon ready.*

CHAPTER TWENTY-SIX

HUMBLE.

D sat on his black Ikea sofa, looked at the time on his cable box, and flipped over to VH1. Before *Mama's Daye* made its debut, a commercial popped up with Lil Daye sitting on a throne, then in a red Ferrari, then on a Japanese motorcycle, and then helming a catamaran. In each incarnation, Lil Daye was accompanied by an unobtainable woman of a different ethnicity and held a bottle of Sinsere. He was lip-synching the words to his single "Toss It Up," inviting folks to enjoy the grand life with every sip. In the final section, Lil Daye sat at the head of a board of directors' table. Mama Daye walked over and poured Sinsere into two tall crystal glasses. The last image showed the digitally enhanced glasses looking like they held golden honey.

Right after the commercial came a high, wide drone shot of an Atlanta McMansion. It zoomed in to a large front door, which opened to reveal Mama Daye, resplendent in a simmering Sinsere-colored gown with a little girl on her hip and a little boy holding onto her leg. Lil Daye walked up the steps, decked out in a white Ducati motorcycle onesie. As the instrumental of "Toss It Up" played, the title card for *Mama's Daye* popped up on-screen. D watched the first scene, in which the Dayes had breakfast and argued over marijuana smoke's impact on the kids. As soon as his executive producer credit appeared, D clicked over to the NBA channel. The enterprising Daye family shot the whole series before they sold it, controlling every frame of the mythmaking process.

Text messages flooded in. Social media was lit with praise, snark, and GIFs. The verdict was that Lil Daye, Mama Daye, and their managers (namely D Entertainment) had pulled off some pop-culture magic, taking the Atlanta MC (and his family) from rap star to pop phenomenon in the space of one TV spot and a half hour of heavily scripted "unscripted" cable.

D sat there a bit stunned. It felt like D Hunter, the Brooklyn security guard/bodyguard/crisis manager, had just died and been reborn as a powerhouse Hollywood manager. It was a heady feeling. Industry heat blazed off his phone like the sun at Joshua Tree.

Then it hit him. D felt fear. Fear that he'd become addicted. Fear that he could never go back. He'd been around other peoples' heat scores of times, so he knew nothing was more fleeting than a sense of total victory. In the moment of triumph, all D could think of was Ice, and Conrad, and the ghosts of the plot against hip hop. His mind wandered to an odd place: the White House. D wondered if Trump, ambling alone past portraits of former leaders at night, recalled all the mean, heartless, and criminal things he'd done in the name of "winning." Did he wait for the bodies of the abused to rise up and grab him? 'Cause D, in this moment of outward triumph, could feel danger nipping his heels like a hungry dog.

CHAPTER TWENTY-SEVEN

N.Y. STATE OF MIND

Maggie rubbed sweat off her forehead with her right hand and flicked it at D while he tried to maintain a straight face. They were breathing deeply in tandem, their bodies wet with moisture as they twisted their limbs and torsos. "Reverse warrior," said the petite blond yoga instructor, and both of them, along with the twenty-five other people in the class, bent backward, one arm reaching for an ankle, the other in the air.

D had practiced yoga for many years, but Maggie had convinced him that "hot" yoga was the next level in terms of increased flexibility and fitness. This was D's second class with her at Modo Yoga. During the last, he'd felt his body overheating, his eyes irritated by dripping sweat; his flexibility left so much to be desired.

But no matter how challenging the class, Maggie was always smiling. She had a cheerleader's wide-eyed animation tempered by a realness that D admired. She'd seen quite a few unpleasant aspects of human nature in LA, but there was an essential goodness to her that cut through that darkness. When he'd told Maggie of his HIV status (apparently dormant, though caution was required), she'd asked a lot of pointed questions about his love life and previous partners. They hadn't yet been lovers, but after kissing deeply one night at a West Hollywood party, D felt he needed to be up front before things escalated.

The HIV revelation had definitely made Maggie take a step back, rightfully so. When she'd invited him to join her for hot yoga that evening, he'd canceled a business dinner. Despite all the buzz about his business and the money coming in, D was lonely. He longed for the stability of a serious relationship.

After class, Maggie suggested they eat at Café Gratitude, a Beverly Hills restaurant for health-conscious yogis with disposable income. D hoped for an intimate conversation about their relationship, but they ran into a couple members of Travis Scott's team and D got sucked into a dialogue about endorsement deals. Then Maggie saw a fellow dancer-turned-actress, and suddenly it was a five-way dinner.

Nas was doing a few of tracks from *Illmatic* at a Hennessy promotional event at a private Hollywood members club called NeueHouse. So despite his still-damp body, D found himself in a crowd of LA industry types listening to "N.Y. State of Mind" with vegan cuisine in his belly. When Nas had released *Illmatic* in '94, it was inconceivable that D would evolve into a talent manager invited to a Hollywood event alongside a woman as beautiful as Maggie.

He watched Maggie sway to the hypnotic DJ Premier production, the piano sample of Joe Chambers's "Mind Rain" fueling the vibe. Maggie knew some (not all) of the words and was mouthing along with Nas, who sported a fresh, deftly tailored beige silk suit onstage. D looked at her with adoration and then with sadness. He whispered to her, "Be right back," and walked out of the ballroom and out of NeueHouse onto Sunset Boulevard.

Nas's song had caused old demons to rise—the insecurity that had defined D's young life swelled up like a storm, reminding him of his brother's death on a nondescript ghetto street corner in a city that never slept, never expressed regret, and never let you forget. Maybe his damn chakras were just too far open. Whatever brought this on, he'd felt uncomfortable in that room. He had so many things to handle. He had New York, specifically Brooklyn, drawing him back to old, unburied drama. If D's life was a play, he could feel his role being rewritten.

CHAPTER TWENTY-EIGHT

WELCOME TO THE JUNGLE

As soon as D landed at JFK, he felt he was in danger. He absolutely loved New York. Whoever he'd become was still rooted in the city's concrete subway rumble and the chatter of 1,001 passing conversations. D had never felt New York's particular energy anywhere else and wondered if an ancient race had left some pulsating orb right where 42nd Street crossed Broadway.

But, like the title of David Cronenberg's film, to D, the city invoked a history of violence. Three dead brothers. Father run off by their ghosts. Mother suffocated by mourning. Then there was D, who for years wore black, even on the hottest summer day, becoming a pallbearer to his own life. So New York, the vibration in his soul, was also the darkness in his heart.

New York was never static. The constant was subways, cars, and people. Then there was the motion of a history that could be as subterranean as the A train and blunt as a *Daily News* headline. He remembered the city when white people fled to Long Island and New Jersey, when ethnic tensions were inflamed by blockbusting. He'd seen the city when Wall Street flourished and coke had been franchised into crack; the money generated created bottle service, champagne rooms, and crack houses.

Later he'd watched Times Square become Disney. AIDS evolve from gay plague to black tragedy. Mayor Michael Bloomberg's stop-and-frisk become a tool for population control. D's old apartment on Seventh Avenue in Manhattan had been located in a two-story building with a bar on the ground floor. Now that structure was gone, replaced by a glass-and-steel high-rise. The current rewhitening of New York was amusing because, in many cases, it was the grandchildren of those who had escaped, returning to the streets their clan had once abandoned.

An Uber SUV awaited him curbside. He was going to Brooklyn, like he had for a lifetime, but the hotel he was heading to had only existed for a few years. It was in "new Brooklyn," and D was from another country.

D sat in the roof bar of his hotel, sipping a green juice, eating a shrimp salad, and watching Manhattan's lights twinkle, when a call came in.

Without any foreplay, D jumped right in: "You got something for me, Amos?"

"I found some things out about agent Conrad. It may be important; it may not."

"Go on."

"It turns out that Conrad was tight with James Comey," Pilgrim said. "They came up together and Conrad was promoted through the ranks by him."

"So you're suggesting he doesn't have much time at the agency 'cause Comey's gone? That he's trying to tie up some loose ends before he goes? Did he and Comey know about what you had Mayer and his ex–partner in crime Jackson doing?"

"I don't have answers, but these guys are kinda like spies. What they show you may not be what you should be looking at."

"That's a riddle, Amos."

Pilgrim sighed like D was a rookie who needed more seasoning.

"What I'm saying is that Conrad may not really be after whoever killed Mayer and that he probably has a deeper agenda."

With a smile in his voice, D said, "He wants me to help get *you?*"

Pilgrim didn't swallow the bait and said evenly, "Could be, but I don't think so. I think he's after bigger fish than me."

"That sounds like wishful thinking."

"I didn't make all the money I've made being wishful, D," Pilgrim replied, sounding cocky as hell. "These FBI people are smart. He wouldn't be meeting with you unless he already knew the answers to whatever questions he's gonna ask you. So this meeting isn't to get facts from you. It's about something else, so prepare yourself. Don't get emotional. Just be calm and call me when it's over."

"Don't get emotional? You don't get to tell me how to act."

"No. I'm just the man advising you." Pilgrim's tone changed. Coming through the phone now was the voice that had closed a thousand deals. "I haven't had a chance to tell you this, but I'm impressed by you, D. Look at your journey. From doorman to bodyguard to manager to dealmaker. You learned from Walter Gibbs, who sat across from me many times seeking advice. Gibbs could have been bigger—bigger than me because of the opportunities that have opened up for black folks. Yet Gibbs, as you well know, he didn't have the laser focus. But you are smart, a learner. Plus, you ain't pussy crazy, which is what pulled Gibbs's ass down. You could be an asset."

"Don't try to mentor me, Amos. We are never gonna have that relationship. Amina is dead because of your moves. I had to kill a man because of you. I'm in shit with this FBI agent because of you. So don't kiss my ass."

"All right," Pilgrim said, clearly miffed. "Just call me after you talk with Conrad."

D clicked off first, satisfied with that small verbal victory over the old man.

CHAPTER TWENTY-NINE
FINESSE

The text was simple and chilling: *I'm back in BK too.* It was from a blocked number, which meant it wasn't Fly Ty or a relative. It meant it was Ice.

Ice in Brooklyn wanting to see D was not a good thing. Not for D. Not for Brooklyn. Not for anyone who Ice felt, rightly or wrongly, threatened by. You never wanted to run into Ice unexpectedly. You wanted every encounter with him to be well-planned and in a brightly lit place.

But that was not to be. "I need to see you tonight," Ice now said over the phone. "I'm going to see someone and you should be there."

"I won't be free until after ten," D said.

"That works. Where you staying? Downtown or Williamsburg?" Ice said *Williamsburg* with a sarcastic inflection, as if the idea of D in hipsterville-turned-yuppieland was a joke.

Confirming Ice's suspicion, D suggested they meet outside the Wythe Hotel across from the Brooklyn Bowl, a block that epitomized the new Brooklyn as much as any. Ice didn't know where that was—he'd left Brooklyn before condo-mania remade WillieB—but said he'd roll through around eleven p.m.

At the appointed hour, D stood in front of the Wythe Hotel, looking over the salt-and-pepper crowd lined up across the street in front of Brooklyn Bowl, where Questlove was doing his weekly residency. It wasn't very many years ago that D would have been standing at the head of the line, checking IDs, shining a flashlight into purses, and keeping an eye out for people on the no-admittance list. D wasn't nostalgic for those nights, but he did marvel at how foreign that life seemed now. It was like standing across from your old high school and remembering squeezing your pimples.

It was in his doorman nights that D came into regular contact with men like Ice. No matter what they wore—tracksuits and Adidas or crisply tailored Armani—their eyes always gave away their souls. Cops' eyes were wary and observational, looking for faces from bulletins. Killers' eyes were different. They saw inside you. They saw your entrails and organs, your veins and muscles. Anything that could be hurt. Anything that would stop you cold.

It was these eyes that gazed at D from the backseat of a black Nissan Rogue before the mouth attached said, "Hop in." In the front seat were two burly black men, one of them in his twenties and driving. A man closer to Ice's age sat in the passenger seat. No introductions were made. The men stayed silent as the car navigated its way across Brooklyn.

Ice asked, "Would you like a pickle?" A jar of pickles sat between his legs.

D declined.

Ice reached down, pulling two moist pickles out of the jar. "Yo," he said to the men up front, "there are only a few left." The two men traded a *Damn, I'm tired of these fucking pickles* look, but those words did not pass their lips. Instead, the man in the passenger seat took the pickles, handing one to the driver.

"D," Ice said, "I know you remember when Junior's used to have a big jar of pickles on every table."

"Yeah," D replied, "they used to have beets and coleslaw in glass jars too."

"Yeah. I used to love eating them pickles. Big and juicy. Liked them better than the cheesecake. People told me I was crazy, but the truth is the truth. Sure you don't want one? Got two left."

The man's jovial storytelling attitude felt creepy to D, like sitting next to a happy grim reaper. "Nawn, Ice. Not hungry. So where are we going?"

"There's a guy here that the FBI agent spoke to. He was once affiliated with me. I don't know what they talked about or how cooperative he was."

"Why am I here, Ice?'

"'Cause you are involved, D. *Very* involved." Ice smiled.

D glanced over at the door even though he knew the child lock was on. "If you plan to murk this man, you can let me out of the car right now."

"No," Ice said calmly. "Ain't nobody gettin' murked tonight." Then he bit into a pickle and looked out the window as the car passed Empire Boulevard in the Caribbean area of Flatbush.

"So," D said, "what are you gonna do, Ice?"

"Ensure our safety." Ice finished his pickle and closed the jar.

D said, "You keep eating those things and you're gonna turn green."

"We all have our vices," Ice said. "So you've been talking to that FBI agent?"

"That's why I'm in Brooklyn. You know that. But I haven't had a sit-down with him yet."

"When's the meet?"

"Tomorrow morning."

"Keep my name out your mouth."

"Of course."

A few more blocks past Empire, the car turned left and rolled by well-maintained brownstones and then made another left, this time onto Rogers Avenue, an architectural dividing line between the brownstones and much less elegant buildings. Rogers was home base to storefront churches, ugly rental apartments, and the odd hipster artisanal coffee shop. They parked in front of an apartment building that defined the word *modest*.

The younger of the two nameless men stepped out of the car and opened the building's front door. Ice got out with the pickle jar still under his arm. He came around and opened D's door. "Don't be rude, D," he said.

The apartment was in the rear on the first floor. The furniture was clean and sparse. A bachelor's place. A blend of curry chicken and roach spray filled the room. A$AP Rocky's voice came through the wall from another apartment. A muffled voice could be heard from the tiny bathroom where the two thugs stood in the doorway. A man sat on the toilet seat with a gag in his mouth. His hands and feet were tied. Sweat streamed down his face. The man's anxious eyes bugged out when Ice entered his vision.

"Long time, Fade," Ice said. "I hear you and the FBI have been talking. No need to deny it. I still have friends in this bitch. Believe that. So what I need to know is what he asked you."

Ice turned and handed the pickle to jar to D. He then moved over to the captive and pulled the gag out of his mouth. "So," he said softly, "let's hear it."

Fade spoke haltingly with a Caribbean accent, though D couldn't place the island. "He wanted to know who this guy Mayer used to buy guns from. He said he thought the man was murdered. Told him I didn't know shit about that. He was here and then he wasn't. Think I worry about some Jew tryin' to act black? I didn't tell him nothing 'cause I know nothing."

"So that was it?"

"That was it, Ice," Fade said shakily.

Ice leaned close, his spittle showering the man's face. "Then why you asking about me at the old-school barbecue? Asking about where I be at? Well, I'm here now. Whatchu wanna know?"

Fade talked fast and furiously: "All I was saying was how dope it would be to see you at that event. Like old times in the hood. That's all. I know better than to be nosy about you."

Ice leaned away from Fade and slowed the pace of his words. "That's sweet of you to remember me. Real sentimental. Except I think that FBI agent offered you something or threatened to pull you into some situation. You felt squeezed. I feel that. But he got to you by asking about me. That concerns me and I don't like being concerned." Ice turned to D and said, "My man."

D handed him the pickle jar.

Ice continued, "Now, I don't like being asked about. It gets people thinking about me and where I'm at . . . All right, flip him."

The two thugs stood Fade up, pulled down his pants and underwear, and shoved him facedown into the tub.

Both Fade and D shouted, "What the fuck?!"

Ice opened the pickle jar. He poured the pungent green pickle juice over the man's backside, then took a pickle in his hand and held it next to the man's face. "You want this?"

"NO! NO! NO!"

"Don't ever talk about me again. I hear about you even saying my name and I'll use more than pickle juice on that ass. You gonna be shitting green. You hear me?"

"YES! YES!"

Ice said, "All right," and the two thugs jerked Fade upright and perched him on the edge of the bathtub. Ice stood in front of his victim and held the pickle an inch from his face. "What is the moral of this story?"

"K-keep your name outta my mouth," Fade stammered.

Ice then tossed the pickle on the floor and walked out.

Back in the car, Ice's two thugs became quite animated, laughing about what they'd just done. Ice didn't say a thing. He just looked out the window at Brooklyn, old and new. D matched his silence.

When D got out of the car, he turned to Ice and said, "Message received."

Ice nodded and the car pulled off.

CHAPTER THIRTY

I FEEL IT COMING

he FBI's main Manhattan office was at 26 Federal Plaza on Broadway near City Hall, but D's meeting with Conrad was a few blocks uptown in a building near Canal Street. This seemed a good sign to D, suggesting that this case wasn't a priority at an investigative agency whose Most Wanted List was filled with cybercrime suspects and violent gang members. A conspiracy against hip hop, even if it led to the murder of an (ex) agent, couldn't be very important in the larger scheme of things. Ex-director James Comey was still in the headlines, and based on Amos's tip, he hoped Conrad was too worried about job security to squeeze D hard.

After he went through security, D sat on a hard plastic chair in a drab bureaucratic room. He looked up at Trump's visage grinning at him next to a drooping American flag. He'd contemplated bringing an attorney but decided to go it alone. Maybe that was misplaced optimism but instinct told him going solo was the best introductory move with Conrad.

Conrad was a ruddy-faced, middle-aged man with red thinning hair, a decent dark-blue suit, and a studious manner. He seemed more of an insurance claims adjuster than a grand inquisitor, but D was aware that real government agents didn't aspire to be James Bond. It was best not to underestimate them. Instead of some institutional-looking interview room, Conrad led him into a small office with bad lighting, cheap-looking furniture, and a boring view of a charmless building across Broadway.

Next to the corner bookshelf was a photo of Conrad and a smiling woman holding an impressive striped bass. The office was otherwise bereft of personal items. Behind the desk, two boxes sat on the windowsill along with several black binders.

After a few pleasantries, Conrad grabbed a binder from one of the boxes, opened to the first page, and began: "Malik Jones broke into your office on Broadway in 2011? Is that correct?"

"Yes."

"Did you know he was a former FBI agent?"

"No. I just knew him as a thug from the West Coast hip hop scene."

Conrad said, "I knew him back when he was still an agent. His transformation was shocking."

"I didn't know about any of that," D said firmly, hoping he wasn't hitting that fiction too hard.

"His real name was Anthony Jackson. You dated his wife."

D lied badly: "What? Who?"

"Amina Jackson. They had been married during his FBI days. We believe Jackson had her murdered to cover his tracks."

"Then," D said slowly, "I should have killed him that night at my office. If I'd known he was behind Amina's death, I would have shown no mercy."

Conrad just looked at D for a beat and then said, "Thankfully, you showed good judgment, Mr. Hunter. I interviewed Jackson at a federal penitentiary two months ago. He asked for me since we'd worked together. He told me an incredible unsubstantiated story about hip hop. I've never been anything but a casual fan. The fact that there were people who thought it corrupted America's young people was hard to believe. Then Jackson directed me to the case of a man named Eric Mayer, another ex-FBI agent who became involved with it. Did you know Eric Mayer?"

"Not well," D said. "I met him a few times through business. I believe he hired my old security company—"

"D Security?"

"Yes, that was the name. I believe he hired us to work an event or two back in the late nineties."

"What did you think of Mayer?"

"Thought he was a wannabe Lyor Cohen."

"Who?"

D decided to provide some hip hop history: "Lyor Cohen. Back in day he managed a lot of hip hop artists. Ran Def Jam during the nineties. Now works for YouTube. Jewish guy—maybe even Israeli—who always got on well with black folks. That's what Mayer aspired to."

"So you didn't have a personal relationship with him?"

"No." This wasn't actually a lie, other than D allowing Ice to kill him.

Conrad reached into a file on his desk, pulled out some papers, and slid them over to D. There were e-mails about D. There were travel itineraries and hotel receipts. There were photos of D outside D Security's old offices in SoHo. There was a sheet with his old Manhattan home address on Seventh Avenue, his D Security business landlines, his old BlackBerry number, and his Social Security number. D flashed back to the NYPD's "hip hop cop," who used to surveil MCs for the police.

"Why do you think he was so interested in you, Mr. Hunter?"

There were a million bad answers to that question and about a half of them passed through D's mind before he parted his lips and told the truth: "Dwayne Robinson."

"The murdered hip hop writer?"

"Dwayne would have said he wrote about black music—African American music—and that hip hop was only the current branch of that tree. He knew about all forms of black music. But let me jump ahead a bit so we don't have to do a long, drawn-out verbal dance."

Conrad seemed a little irritated by D's tone. But staying professional, he just crossed his hands and said, "Please, Mr. Hunter, go on."

"Dwayne was working on a book called *The Plot Against Hip Hop* when he was murdered. I never saw the whole manuscript, 'cause it was stolen after he died. But I know that Mayer was someone Dwayne thought was destructive to hip hop culture and that he had a chapter in the book outlining the reasons why."

Conrad took this in and then asked, "How does that explain his interest in *you?*"

"I was close with Dwayne," D explained. "He was my mentor. I wouldn't be doing the things I now do in business without his guidance. Mayer must have known that. Maybe he was afraid of me and wanted to find some dirt. In truth, I don't really wanna know."

Conrad nodded. "Glad you are so forthcoming, Mr. Hunter. You say you've never read the manuscript?"

"Only bits and pieces. But D told me a lot about what he was trying to do."

Conrad reached down, pulled a cardboard box out of a leather bag, and placed it on the table. "Take a look."

D gasped. He hadn't expected this. "Is this the manuscript?"

"It is. There are a couple of chapters I'd like your feedback on." Conrad pulled out a paper-clipped chapter and handed it to D. "Give it a read. I'll call you in two hours. I think you'll get through these pages fast."

D picked up the box, and a moment later he was tearing up.

Conrad watched him dispassionately. "Please feel free to take it with you. Let's speak in two hours," he said.

D wiped his eyes and left the room in silence.

CHAPTER THIRTY-ONE

ON TO THE NEXT ONE

D sat at a table in Hampton Chutney, an Indian dosa joint in SoHo that had been his go-to spot back in the day. He was buried in the thoughts of a dead writer. Dwayne Robinson wrote:

There are many popular conspiracy theories related to hip hop. One of the most popular is about a "secret meeting" redirecting hip hop into its gangsta rap era, as if the culture's embrace of crack narratives started on the West Coast or that hip hop could be controlled top-down when all its innovations, themes, and techniques flowed from the street.

If you were going to control hip hop from the outside, it would have to be done inside out, like a bug buried deep in a computer program that would slowly subvert the system. And that is exactly what is happening. Hip hop, being an agile beast, has leaped in and out of outsider's clutches.

However, these agent provocateurs are around and they are busy building their own empires, not simply to make money, but to serve the goals of those who care little for the culture and the community that nurtured it.

The central figure in the plot against hip hop is a man named Samuel Kurtz, CEO of Diversified International Brands and owner of a plethora of other companies. In 2009, he spoke at the Culture and Conscience Conference in Boca Raton, Florida, to about twenty people in a conference room at the Boca Raton Resort & Club Hotel. Unknown to Kurtz, someone recorded his remarks. I purchased a copy of the transcript for five hundred dollars from someone who attended the meeting. I have heard the actual tape but was not allowed to have a copy. This is legit.

For all you hip hop conspiracy folks, here you go. For all of you who don't believe in conspiracies, I hate to open your eyes but this is the blue pill. At the conference, Samuel Kurtz gave a talk called "The Sociocultural Tools of Neoconservative Capitalism."

Kurtz's opening remarks concerned hip hop as a marketing tool. "When this hip hop thing first caught on, it appalled me. It was loud, too ghetto, and seemed dangerous for the country. Then when Run-D.M.C. made a very effective sneaker deal with Adidas, I realized that this thing was an advertising delivery system. It sold ideas, attitudes, and products. Its words went right into the consciousness of the listeners. Unlike advertising, where there can be resistance and tuning out, rap was readily accepted and rappers were natural product endorsers and spokespeople."

This is eerie, D thought. Kurtz had said the same thing to these neocons that he'd said in the meeting with D. *Am I, in my eagerness to make a big deal, as greedy and mean as this bunch?*

But then, instead of hyping his new beverage, Kurtz's remarks took a sinister turn:

"The promotion of very narrow values in hip hop music goes hand in hand with targeted government policies. In turn, they can create extremely lucrative business opportunities for us. The street-drug cul-

ture that hip hop glamorizes, and in many cases is funded by, leads to arrests and incarceration. Investments in the private prison industry have been bolstered by the laws passed at the height of the nineties crack economy (one thing we can actually thank the Clintons for)."

This last comment received loud, sarcastic laughter from the collected fat cats. Kurtz continued: "Minimum mandatory sentencing turned our speculation in private prisons into cash cows that have transformed so many American towns, generating jobs in a wide spectrum of businesses while throwing off dollars that turn into cashflow funds that help elect politicians who support our ideas. It has been a perfect storm.

"Going forward, I am investing in charter schools. The goal here is to both run education more efficiently, but also to control the information about American values that are inculcated. In addition, the removal of resources from public education is a direct way to keep large percentages of minority children on the school-to-prison pipeline, which fills our private prisons and allows us to tap into a huge supply of low-cost labor for decades to come. The public sector pays for the care and feeding of the incarcerated workers. The profits generated flow to prison owners, vendors, and the companies' contracts to have their products made. Even in the face of automated factories of the future, the cost efficiency of the incarcerated will be hard to beat.

"Another link in this chain is that the more minorities who are in jail, the fewer who have the right to vote. This is crucial in states and districts where the white-vs.-minority count is close and the balance of power can be swung. Disenfranchising thousands of voters can be key in keeping our candidates in office and our agenda moving forward.

"Right now I am extremely bullish on alcohol and energy drinks. Cheap alcoholic beverages laced with high levels of sugar and packaged in the colors of children's candy are a huge focus for my company in the years ahead. Linked with the right pop culture or music figures, it can generate substantial profits and increase petty crime rates, which helps both our financial and political goals."

After Kurtz finished his horrifying vision of how hip hop could be a tool in the enslavement of a generation of minority youth, applause burst from his listeners. Then they broke for lunch. On the afternoon agenda were remarks by Dinesh D'Souza on making right-wing documentaries and Coachella owner Philip Anschutz of AEG on turning left-wing culture into right-wing income. For these businessmen/activists pushing a right-wing agenda, hip hop was not a revolutionary opposition. It was a world of small-time musicians who could be tools to help maintain the master's house. They were mental slaves to the rhythm of capitalism. But what Kurtz didn't say is that his involvement with hip hop didn't end with liquor deals and ad campaigns. The truth was, Kurtz wanted a way to steer the culture and tamp down its progressive tendencies. He found the most unlikely collaborators in that (mis)adventure.

D set the manuscript aside, took another bite of his dosa, and looked out on Grand Street. He could see where this was going. He knew this part of the tale all too well. The only mystery that remained was why Amos Pilgrim collaborated with Samuel Kurtz. D continued reading:

Amos Pilgrim is a legend in the music business. He is not simply a talent manager and label owner, but a connector of people, jobs, and money. His name comes up in a variety of contexts, doing a variety of things. But no one has ever accused Pilgrim of being a crook, which, in the music business, is an amazing accomplishment. In all my years covering the music industry, I've never heard a discouraging word aimed at Amos Pilgrim. He is more than respected. He is beloved.

At some point in the early nineties, Pilgrim realized that hip hop was no longer a subgenre. It was going to dominate black music, which meant it would eventually dominate American music and then the world, just as jazz, rock and roll, disco, and other black music had before. Pilgrim got it in his head that he should control hip hop, or at least have a strong grip on its lever so he could direct it and fulfill his neoliberal agenda.

At the Ivy in Beverly Hills in the summer of 1993, Pilgrim and Kurtz had dinner. On the agenda was a promotional deal involving various black advertising agencies and Kurtz's brands. But that was just the excuse for two businessmen to have a wide-ranging conversation about political and cultural trends. Pilgrim was on the board for a couple of Kurtz's businesses, while Kurtz had contributed generously to several charities that Pilgrim supported. They were people who had money, made each other more money, embraced each other's charitable ventures, and enjoyed sitting and trading visions for the nation.

So Pilgrim told Kurtz of his plan to plant agents in hip hop's East and West Coast scenes to steer them in specific directions, with a special emphasis on co-opting the volatile, charismatic Tupac Shakur, whose family has a political background and links to important figures on both coasts. Kurtz was fascinated and offered his assistance, suggesting that operatives trained in surveillance, counterintelligence, and undercover ops would be necessary to fulfill Pilgrim's vision. Kurtz put Pilgrim in contact with executives at

White Cube, an organization with both aboveground online digital intelligence and underground tactical intelligence.

With White Cube's help, Pilgrim was able to identify several Federal Bureau of Investigation agents to be recruited. After a year of background checks and an ample financial offer, two FBI agents—Eric Mayer and Anthony Jackson, a.k.a. Malik Jones— joined Pilgrim's project. Technically speaking, Mayer and Jackson/ Jones both resigned from the Bureau. According to files obtained via the Freedom of Information Act, both men had taken early retirement to work in private security. In fact, both used a Kurtz holding company as their forwarding address.

I believe they never fully left the FBI. Even as they reported to Pilgrim, they passed along information about hip hop figures (who, in the eyes of many in the FBI, were all associated with drug traffickers) to law enforcement. They also funneled information to Kurtz that helped the marketing of various consumer products. In the first two years of this operation, Pilgrim received regular updates on their activities and they often made moves based on his orders.

Eventually or, perhaps given the nature of hip hop, unavoidably, by year three, both agents went rogue. Each chose a side in the East Coast/West Coast rap war of the midnineties, losing contact with their original selves in the fractured dual-identity dreamscape of hip hop. They lived their own real-life gangsta videos. Soon, they were gunning for each other as if they were rival rap moguls. How this affected their contact with the FBI is unfortunately unclear, but their fixation on Tupac did continue. In fact, Mayer was traveling to the Upstate New York prison where Tupac was held in 1996, arriving a day after Suge Knight and attorney David Kenner made their infamous jailhouse deal with the MC.

I can't confirm with absolute certainty that Mayer and Jackson/ Jones played a role in the assassinations of the Notorious B.I.G. and Tupac. They weren't triggermen. They didn't order either shot. But both were trained in subversion and innuendo. Both understood the art of misdirection. There is no doubt in my mind that using the tools employed against Dr. Martin Luther King, the Black Panthers, and many black elected officials, these two men helped inflame the climate that resulted in the culture-altering shootings in Las Vegas and Los Angeles.

Only after these deaths did Pilgrim realize how out of control it had all become. While this carnage brought sorrow to Pilgrim, to Kurtz it meant opportunity. During the nineties, he began shifting from a moderate, business-oriented Republican to an increasingly conservative position, heightened by demographic surveys that predicated a browner America in the twenty-first century. Looking at Kurtz's companies from the outside, you'd never have known this. His alcohol, beverage, and clothing ventures made plentiful use of African American pop culture.

But in meetings like the one quoted earlier in this chapter, Kurtz developed a nefarious vision of how the raw parts of this culture could further his overall political agenda. His investments in private prisons and charter schools coalesced under one big idea: limiting minority social advancement would solidify white control of America, despite unfavorable demographics. Where Pilgrim wanted to harvest hip hop as a fresh field for political engagement, Kurtz used it as a tool to manipulate both creators and consumers, guiding them toward thinking and modes of behavior that supported the goals of white supremacy.

CHAPTER THIRTY-TWO

FLASHING LIGHTS

D sat on a bench in Washington Square Park watching a guitar player perform the Beatles' "Blackbird" with more intention than success. It had been a long while since D had chilled in this park, the site of many conversations, kisses, herb purchases, and late-night pissing bouts against trees. In keeping with the general upgrades around New York, the once-dormant fountain was spouting lovely plumes of water into the Greenwich Village sky as NYU students, marijuana sellers, dog walkers, homeless men, and lovers strolled, stumbled, wandered, and held hands as New Yorkers had in this park for decades.

He saw Conrad walking toward him under the Washington Square Arch, looking quite relaxed for a man who had been handling explosive (written) material earlier. Perhaps that was why the agent's gait seemed soft and easy. He'd shared his big secret. It was D's time to be uptight. "Why did you give me those chapters?"

"You follow the news, Mr. Hunter? What's been going on at the FBI?"

"To me it's all a jumble. But if I'm not mistaken, it looks like the FBI is standing up to Trump."

"Some elements are in that camp." Conrad spoke very deliberately. If D had been slightly patronizing in describing the music world, Conrad took a more educational tone in giving D insight into the inner workings of the Bureau. "Many good people just think the law is more important than one man. When it comes to instances of black militancy, however, ppeople believe the agency is well served by being aggressive in domestic counterintelligence. As you should know, but perhaps don't, the Justice Department has a mandate to undermine what they define as black extremist groups."

D wanted to jump all over Conrad. He'd seen enough documentaries on the Black Panthers to know that the FBI's record of investigating/subverting black activist organizations was dark and nasty. But he needed information, so he tried not to sound accusatory when he asked, "We talking Black Lives Matter, right?"

"That is absolutely one group that is being scrutinized," Conrad said without a shred of embarrassment. "So the subversion described in Robinson's manuscript isn't new, but it's not quite old either. What Robinson outlines is a connection between business and government to use culture as a tool of population control, something I've seen before. It is my belief that government should not be employed as an extension of a corporation. Others may not share that view, but I believe it is an essential tenet of our democracy."

"You should tell #45 that."

Conrad smiled tightly. "Obviously, I'm not someone with a lot of influence."

D said, "But Mayer and Jackson were out of the Bureau when they got into the hip hop business."

"I think the book makes a strong enough case for the ongoing relationship between Jackson, Mayer, and the Bureau that it will make a big splash, and that splash is why I shared it with you."

So there it is, D thought. *This isn't about implicating me. It's about using me to release this info. Using me as a tool.*

"No one at the Bureau knows about the manuscript, Mr. Hunter," Conrad assured him. "There's no paper trail there."

"So your investigation has been off the books?"

"That is correct."

"So you've been scaring the fuck out of me on a personal mission? You saying I'm in no legal jeopardy?"

"Listen," Conrad said, trying to inject some warmth into the conversation, "I had to see who you were. I knew you were close friends with Robinson, but when you cried over the manuscript, I knew you cared enough to do what should be done."

"And that is?"

"Someone needs to fulfill the destiny of this man's research. I can't do that. I don't really know how."

"Plus," D said, "your fingerprints on this would end your FBI career."

"Sir," Conrad responded with a shrug, "my career at the Bureau is over. I am perceived as close to Comey by the administration and I'm going to be a sacrificial lamb to calm the savage beast. Comey is radioactive to many in the government, which makes me toxic. I'm taking early retirement. So, Mr. Hunter, I am almost out the door."

"Hell of a goodbye present to the FBI."

"That's not what this is about." For the first time since they'd met, Conrad actually seemed a bit passionate. "This is a way for you to honor your mentor's work. I know you want to do that. Make sure he didn't die in vain."

D gazed at corny-ass Conrad and realized this guy was kind of playing him, trying to convince D to do something dangerous, something that could get him killed. "So you wanna use me to get revenge on someone, huh?"

"I'm helping you shed light on a dark corner of American history. Now, if you don't want to do that because you are afraid, that's understandable."

D tossed that back, saying, "You know your name could still come up. I'm not a journalist. I have no obligation, no oath that tells me to protect my sources."

"I don't think you collaborating with an FBI agent would help your cause, Mr. Hunter," Conrad replied smugly. "In fact, I would suggest the narrative is that you found this lost manuscript among Robinson's old papers. Of course you felt obligated to use it to help shine a light on the forces trying to destroy hip hop. The former FBI agents are dead. Kurtz is very much alive. You could damage his business deeply and perhaps bring attention to his connection to the president's men. I think that would be a worthwhile endeavor, Mr. Hunter. Don't you?"

Conrad reached into his pocket, handed D a thumb drive, then stood up and walked away.

Dwayne Robinson's manuscript could be the Pentagon Papers of hip hop, D thought. *But would the* New York Times *or the* Washington Post *care about this?* He needed a strategy, one that got the word out but somehow protected him from blowback.

When D got back to the hotel, the first thing he did was make copies of the key pages in the hotel's business office. Then he went up to the hotel's rooftop, pulled out a Cuban cigar, and lit it as he peered out at the New York skyline. This view would have been impossible just five years before. Few buildings in Brooklyn had been built this high for most of the borough's history. Where D now stood would have been the air high above a hot dog stand or a vendor hawking incense and house music tapes. The past was on the ground, the present in the sky.

Maybe it would be best not to take Conrad's bait. Mayer was dead. Jackson/Jones was in jail. Dwayne Robinson was dead. So were Tupac, Biggie, and a lot of other people who fit into the manuscript's narrative.

They had all died before hip hop won, had all been buried or cremated years before the phrase "hip hop billionaire" wasn't just a brag on vinyl. Would posting the contents of the thumb drive mean anything today?

D worried that the past would consume him like a fire in a housing project, racing up and down elevator shafts, using the incinerator garbage as fuel before torching every man, woman, and child. His fire had been the murder of his three brothers back when hoods were still called ghettos and black people weren't African Americans. The shootings of Matty, Rashid, and Jah had basically shaped his whole life. The murders had broken his mother, driven his father into exile, and conspired to transform D into a low-key vigilante. There was a gaping hole in D Hunter that he'd tried filling by saving people 'cause he'd been too young to save his brothers.

And what had that past done for him? Had he ever been his own person, or was his life just a reaction to the past, not a creation of his free will? Somewhere in the distance, as D now looked east from the roof deck, were the Tilden housing projects where he'd been raised and his brothers gunned down. *If we remain trapped by the past, what kind of future can we make? Aren't we doomed to reflect past tragedies, seeing everything though a prism that limits new possibilities?* D needed to think about what to do, and not just react.

There was, however, one move he felt compelled to make now.

Around midnight he made the call. She was shocked and excited when D gave her the overview and said he'd be over with the manuscript in the morning. He hadn't been over to the Robinson's house in Jersey since the wake several years earlier. He'd seen Dwayne's widow quite a few times since then, but always in Manhattan at a dinner or event where Dwayne was being remembered. D had attended many

Sunday dinners and Saturday barbecues there in previous years, but after Dwayne's murder, the house felt haunted to him.

But this was different. He was bringing Dwayne's ghost with him.

It didn't take long for Danielle's tears to flow. Just looking at the 350-page manuscript on her coffee table made her cry. The dedication, *To my enduring love, Dede*, made her sob. It wasn't until later, after her tears had dried and tea had been served, that Danielle said, "So, this is why my husband was killed?"

D explained, as best he could, the impact that the publication of *The Plot Against Hip Hop* would have had then, and could still have now.

"Are you in danger?" she asked.

"Not necessarily from the FBI, but from people who are afraid of the unknown. Who knows what will come out once people start digging? The book isn't definitive proof of anything, but it's like a hole in a dike. Once water starts seeping out, people may drown. Someone might see killing me as a life preserver."

"I'm afraid for you, D. These are crazy times."

"I know. I'm not sure yet how to put this out, or even if it makes sense to do that. But whatever decision I make, I'll let you know."

Now it was D's turn to cry.

CHAPTER THIRTY-THREE

TEARS DRY ON THEIR OWN

D hadn't been to the Brownsville funeral home in nearly twenty years. Back in the nineties, that Brooklyn institution had been a depressingly regular destination, after crack madness had turned the streets of Brownsville (and all of America's Brownsvilles) into shooting galleries. Greed, addiction, and unemployment created a trilogy of terror that made ghetto undertakers rich.

So much death. It was the legacy that drove D to favor a black wardrobe (though no longer every day). Today, D was back at his old hood's busiest funeral home because of the another nineties scourge—the AIDS epidemic. D wasn't sure how he'd gotten HIV, but he suspected it came from LaWanda Jackson who'd also been messing with a fool named Lee Lee, who had been messing with the white girl, a.k.a. heroin. Lee Lee had likely been sharing needles with infected addicts. D figured he'd been at the far end of the daisy chain, one that was still hard to track since LaWanda had been a carrier who hadn't shown any symptoms.

That was until, all these years later, LaWanda had suddenly died of pneumonia. She had always been in denial of her role in D's infection. As far as D could piece together from mutual friends and relatives, when her temperature fluctuated and her bowels loosened, LaWanda locked into a conviction that she wasn't HIV positive. To admit her condition would have made her complicit in infecting D (and perhaps others).

Her health had fallen apart fast in the last four months, but D had only been contacted when his old lover was near death. It was just a strange coincidence that D was in Brooklyn the night of her wake. He'd delayed his flight back to LA to attend and had a car waiting outside the funeral home to whisk him to JFK. He had no bitterness toward her. They had gotten together in the days when sex, no matter how good, could lead to death, and they'd walked that tightrope together.

As D moved up the viewing room's center aisle, he felt a heavy presence. In a funeral home, it's hard to be spooked by death since death there is like water to a fish—one doesn't exist without the other. However, the usual funeral home death essence was spiced today with a restlessness unavailable to the dead.

D gazed down at LaWanda, who still looked lovely, and then turned around, where his eyes met Ice, who sat just a few feet away. There was no steel, amusement, or swagger in this killer's eyes. This wasn't the other night's Ice. D sat down next to his acquaintance and coconspirator.

"We go back," Ice said in response to D's question about his presence. "You're from the Ville. I'm from the Ville. LaWanda was from the Ville. You know how that goes."

"Did you go out with her?"

"Why do you care?" Ice snarled.

"She gave me HIV."

The hit man's body stiffened. D was amused at Ice's shock.

"You know that for sure?"

"Not for sure, but I believe it's true."

Ice took this in. He sat quiet. He looked at the coffin. He asked, "You knew Lee Lee?"

"No," D said, "but I know *of* him."

"He did some things for me, before H took him out."

"So you know why I think what I think."

Ice acknowledged the truth of this observation, then moved on. La-Wanda was dead. Lee Lee too. He and D had life to deal with. "I didn't come here to talk to you, but now that you're here, we do need to talk. Let's go outside and not disrespect LaWanda with our bullshit."

Outside of the funeral home, a black Escalade awaited D.

"So," Ice said, "you were headed to LA without talking to me?"

"There was nothing to say."

Ice chuckled. After glancing around to see if anyone was listening, he leaned toward D as he had poor Fade. "You know, I just got an idea: if I put a bullet in you, it would put us both out of our misery. I could leave you right here on the sidewalk and save the staff a long trip west."

"You got a cold sense of humor," D said, though both men knew this was not a joke.

"But you got the monster, huh? I guess that's why you always try to act so fearless. I think I finally understand your ass, D. But putting that aside, did the FBI man ask about me?"

"No," D said. "Not a sentence. Truth is, he's not really after Mayer's killer. Mayer was a rogue agent doing bad things and using FBI resources. The agency doesn't want that out."

"So why's he in Brooklyn diggin' then?"

"I think that's window dressing. He is pushing me to do something. I may wanna do it, but I'm gonna think through all the ramifications. But it doesn't involve you."

Ice was not convinced. "Think. You got a white man—an FBI agent—with an agenda, and you think it'll work for you? You sound real stupid right now."

"Just be patient," D said. "You've been lying low. Stay that way. I remember our visit the other night. I'm in no hurry to eat any pickles."

"You know I respect you, D," Ice said with actual warmth. "Even more now. That's real—no bullshit. But this shit makes me nervous."

An opening. A bit of shared humanity. D said, "You're back in Brooklyn coming out of a wake for a woman we both had feelings for. I know you don't feel comfortable."

"Motherfucker, you got jokes, huh?"

"So whatcha gonna do?"

"I dunno, man," Ice said. "You a loose end. This Conrad is a loose end." He paused. "Maybe I'll see you soon. I know those HIV pills are expensive."

Ice went back inside the funeral home and D got into his ride. Both knew they had a lot of thinking to do.

CHAPTER THIRTY-FOUR
SAY HELLO

Pablo was sitting on a bench next to the baseball field at Brownsville's Betsy Head Park when Ice walked up. Ice had been standing by the elevated train pillars that ran up and down Livonia Avenue. This had once been Ice's turf. Just a block away were the Marcus Garvey projects where he and his crew once held sway. Ice tried not to give into nostalgia but he smiled when the number 3 roared overhead. Those steel train wheels were like a lullaby. It was too quiet in Atlanta. It was too quiet everywhere but here.

Ice had watched Pablo sip coconut water for thirty minutes before deciding it was safe to go over.

Pablo was round, light brown, had been down with Ice for years, and had done some gangsta shit back in the day. Now he was just Ice's eyes and ears, a collector of old debts and new information.

Ice sat down. "Your message said a call came in. How'd they know to call you?"

"He didn't say," Pablo answered. Then he added, "I mean he didn't answer when I asked. It had been awhile since I'd gotten a call. I told him you were dead."

"But they didn't care, huh? Kick it."

"They told me the number. A big bag. Three times your old regular fee." Pablo paused, looking nervous. "Thing is, you know the target."

"Oh." Ice knew a lot of people, so this didn't phase him.

Pablo pulled out his phone and handed it over. When Ice saw D Hunter's picture on the screen, he felt a chill. It wasn't anticipation of the hunt. Not this time.

It was fear. Real fear. *This is a goddamn setup,* he thought. *They know I'm linked to D. They know I may wanna kill him.* (In fact, Ice had been thinking about this a lot.)

NYPD might have lost track of him and buried Mayer as a cold case, but the feds had the resources to find him. His tracks weren't that well covered and his crew was certainly susceptible to indictment. D had gone Hollywood. He may have been from the Ville; his brothers may have died here, true. But now he had a lot to lose. Lil Daye's face was on billboards all over the hood. D's bag was big now. Big enough to do whatever he had to do to protect it.

Whoever made this offer thought the fee would make Ice's decision easy. Problem was, whoever "they" were, they knew way too much about Ice and his history. They knew his contacts.

They might even know where I live, Ice thought. *D isn't just in danger from me. I'm in danger too even if I do kill him, and definitely if I don't.*

So Ice told Pablo, "Tell them it's good as done. When the money comes in, you keep it and then get the fuck out of Brooklyn."

"What?"

"Grab your kids, your woman, and all the shit you can carry, and make a move. Go to PR or something. These people will either turn us in or kill us themselves."

Pablo couldn't believe what Ice was saying. He was in a park but he looked around frantically like the walls were closing in on him. "Fuck, how you know that?"

"'Cause that's what I'd do." Ice stood up and walked away.

CHAPTER THIRTY-FIVE

YOU KNOW I'M NO GOOD

D was in an Uber from LAX to his Miracle Mile apartment when his smartphone buzzed. He'd flown in on the overnight and slept surprisingly well, but when he saw who was calling, he felt irritated, as if he hadn't slept a wink. *Damn, this motherfucker is tracking my moves.* "Good morning," he said to Amos Pilgrim.

"You didn't call me." The old man was unhappy.

"Had a lot on my mind," D deflected.

"Do tell."

"Well, it wasn't anything he said or asked. It's what I read. He had a copy of Dwayne Robinson's book."

"The *Plot* book?"

"Yeah," D said, "Conrad had a copy."

Pilgrim grunted into the phone. "Sounds like we should meet up."

"Yup. Your usual spot? How's nine a.m.?"

"Make it ten."

"Okay."

When D arrived at the Four Seasons, Pilgrim was talking to a young black waiter with a woolly natural. Pilgrim was saying, "This man here is who you should be talking to. D manages Lil Daye and a bunch of other rappers."

"Hello, sir," the waiter said in a respectful tone with a hint of the Virginia/North Carolina. "I'm an MC. My stage name is Tayris Smooth.

I have a show coming up. I know who Mr. Pilgrim is and I wanted to offer him a ticket to my show, but I'd be honored if you or someone from your staff could come." The MC had a relaxed confidence that D vibed with. He gave Tayris Ray Ray's Instagram handle and said to DM him the details.

"No matter how big you get, you gotta keep your eyes on the future," Pilgrim said after the waiter/MC had walked off. "So I assume I'm in the book?"

D sat down. "You know you are. But what I didn't know was that Samuel Kurtz was deeply involved in your bullshit as well."

"If Dwayne Robinson was as good a reporter as you think, he'd know Kurtz ended up driving that thing. Not me."

D was about to respond when an older man's voice cut in: "Am I late?" Edgecombe Lenox was an old-school record man who D thought of as almost godlike among the R&B cats in New York before hip hop washed that world away.

"Of course," Pilgrim said. "Sit your ass down."

Edge, as he was known, slowly eased his nearly eighty-year-old bones into the booth next to Pilgrim. He was dressed like an old bluesman in a dark-brown suit, beige shirt, brown tie, and matching fedora. His long boney fingers held more rings than was practical. He had a gray mustache as long as his mouth (which was saying something) and a big nose upon which brown-tinted shades rested snugly. Why was he here?

"There's a thing that happens when I sit down that messes with me like I can't even begin to describe," Edge began. "It really fuckin' hurts. I have to catch my breath."

"Doctors," Pilgrim said. "They have this person called a doctor. You heard of them? D-O-C-T-O-R. You can spell, right?"

"Fuck you."

"No, fuck *you*," Pilgrim said. "If you won't see a doctor, then don't complain about pain. Pain is an announcement to your brain that the engine needs a tune-up. Even *I* have that figured out."

Edge replied, "I know what's wrong with me. I don't need no doctor running up a bill, messing with my co-pay, and having me take all kinds of pills. I know how they do. Oxy this and Oxy that. Have you meowing like a motherfucking cat."

"Rhymes," Pilgrim chuckled. "You got rhymes now? How about a rhyme about how you're too cheap to see a doctor. Put a couplet on that, man."

"I'm not too cheap," Edge countered. "I'm just too smart. If I don't move that part of my body a certain way, I'm good. I get where I'm going and see who I gotta see with no pills, doctor bills, or medical forms. Sometimes I have some discomfort, but otherwise I'm a free motherfucker. I'm not tied down to prescriptions and a bunch of pills that keep me doped up like a Nebraska redneck."

"Alvin Briggs."

"Yeah?"

"Alvin Briggs," Pilgrim repeated. "You know the name."

"What's he got to do with the price of tea in China?"

"Pneumonia. Died of pneumonia last winter. Hadn't been heard from in a week. Hadn't turned up at his job. Kicked down his door and found him on his sofa. Online racing forms on his laptop. Alvin was only a little younger than us. Dead as day-old beer."

"That's got nothing to do with me. Don't compare me to that fat motherfucker. When he let himself go, he was destined to die early. Fat as he got, Alvin probably *wanted* to go. Saw him one night at a restaurant eating fried chicken, having two screwdrivers, and a slice of cherry pie at eleven p.m., and *then* went to go gambling. Don't compare me to that fool."

They'd been talking as if D weren't at the table. Now Edge motioned with his hand and said, "Anyway, is this young motherfucker trying to blackmail you?"

Pilgrim said, "I'm not sure if he even knows what he wants."

"Whoa," D said, "I'm not trying extort money from anyone."

"No, nigga," Edge said, "I got your number. You think you saving black music, right?"

"I'm just trying to save myself and understand what Amos was doing with Kurtz."

"How you gonna separate yourself from us?"

"What do you mean *us?*"

Edge said, "You think this fool here made these moves by himself? We were all concerned about hip hop. We were hopeful and afraid of it too. We saw it was gonna take over. We'd lived through bebop and rock and roll and soul and funk and damn disco. We knew shit changes. We just thought we could make change on *our* terms."

D was shocked. "You were in on hiring Mayer and Jackson?"

"Me. Amos. A bunch of people whose names you know. It wasn't just this man here. It was a community of black people trying to do our best for black people."

"Then why involve Kurtz?"

"That was my fault," Pilgrim said.

"Dwayne Robinson wrote that you partnered with him and then he took it over."

"Something like that."

D said, "You let a white man hijack your plot. I mean, it was a wack idea anyway and then you let a racist take it over."

"Remember when you punched me at my house?" Pilgrim said. "You broke my jaw, D. But I deserved it. I know all the deaths that happened were my fault. I know that."

"So what is this?" D said. "A pity party? I'm supposed to forget that Dwayne died uncovering your stupid plan and give you some kind of pass 'cause you're old black men?"

"If I'm not mistaken," Edge replied, "you're in business with Kurtz right now."

"That's not gonna stop me from doing the right thing."

"Lil Daye wants you to put out Robinson's book?" Pilgrim asked.

"That's between me and him."

"Fair enough," Edge said. "Amos, you got a car waiting for me?"

"It should be right out front."

"Good meeting you again, D. I've been hearing a lot about you. Keep what we told you in mind and you'll do what's best." Edge wobbled out of the restaurant without a cane, trying his best to walk upright despite his many ailments.

D watched him until he disappeared. "Where's he live?"

"Florida. I knew we were gonna meet when you got back, so I flew him in. He wanted to have his say. Now I wanna talk about *your* life. You know who's president, right? Kurtz and Trump are tight. He was with Trump when he went on that infamous trip to Russia where the president didn't get peed on. Well, you know how Kurtz gets down. You think those guys were celibate in the country that refined human trafficking? So what I suggest is you have someone sweep your office for bugs. Hire a hacker to look at all your computers and your phones. You may wanna reveal that info, but Kurtz is connected to Trump. Trump knows hip hop is powerful and he fears it. He fears it for the reasons all these white men do—it reaches young white people like nobody's business. Maybe he and Kurtz were both in on it. It ain't the worst fight to be in, but you definitely could get bloody. Try not to bring down too many old black men. Anyway, my next meeting is here."

It was Belinda Bowman, the attorney D had met with Pilgrim before. This time she was polite but a little distant, like charming D was no longer essential. Her demeanor suggested serious business was to be discussed.

D was dazed as he waited outside the Four Seasons for his Uber. When he was a bodyguard, the decisions he'd made had been simple. *That woman is okay. That guy over there is a nuisance. That character in the corner is a threat. Keep your eye on him.* He'd enjoyed protecting people. It gave purpose to his life. Who deserved protection now?

CHAPTER THIRTY-SIX
MASK OFF

D had just finished a Zoom videoconference call with a *Billboard* reporter doing a profile of D Management when an e-mail appeared in his inbox. There was another call happening in ten minutes to connect Night with the black activist group Color of Change about performing at their next benefit. But the title of the e-mail, *KURTZ TALK*, and the sender, ME@hiphopcointelpro.org, demanded attention. The message read, *This could be the missing piece of the puzzle or one more reason not to sleep well at night. Probably both.*

Hiphopcointelpro had been the name of a blog run by Truegod, a conspiracy theorist living in a tenement in yet-to-be-gentrified Harlem. Through Truegod, a deeply paranoid and excitable man, D had learned much about the Sawyer memorandum, a marketing plan that had served as a partial blueprint for the plot against hip hop. If D had doubted the plot or questioned Truegod's sanity, he got his answer when the blogger was murdered within minutes of their meeting. So who was using the blog's name now and what was in this video file?

The video was static camera video of the presentation Samuel Kurtz had made in Boca Raton, Florida. It was the same talk Dwayne Robinson described in his manuscript. D had somehow found Kurtz's words. Here now were the accompanying images: a young, tanned businessman in a green Izod shirt and beige slacks in a conference room standing before a whiteboard with the names of various alcohol brands and hip hop figures scrawled in black, blue, and green. D was going to miss his planned phone call.

D had read the chapter in Dwayne Robinson's book, but watching Kurtz lay out his strategy made D feel like throwing up. This video verified Robinson's findings. Had he seen this and taken notes or had he transcribed it himself? The manuscript never mentioned a video. Someone had held onto this video for years and had decided to pass it on to D and not post it on the Internet.

Guess it sat in some GOP archive, D thought. *Had Truegod been a disloyal Republican? It had to have come from someone who knew I was in business with Kurtz. It was sent to force my hand. Could have come from Conrad. Could have come from Amos. Use me to mess with Kurtz. Or was it a test by Amos to see what kind of man I really am?* If he ignored this and didn't tell Lil Daye, then he was a businessman who could be trusted. The tape was a provocation.

D had been wrestling with what to do with the info in Dwayne Robinson's book since he got back to LA. He'd doubted that Lil Daye would read the chapter. He couldn't get the MC to read film scripts with multimillion-dollar offers attached, so there was little chance of getting him to focus on a semischolarly book that called his financial benefactor a racist. D doubted Mama Daye would check it out and Ant was out of the question. D could have tried to talk them through it, but the devil was in the details and he worried that Lil Daye's camp would dismiss it as a dead man's crazy talk.

But a video? Lil Daye would watch this. D was sure that even five minutes of it would impact the MC. Then, together, they could figure out their next move.

Through D's window, smog created a gray veil over Los Angeles.

Another day, another hundred thousand lungs damaged. Time to make that call.

CHAPTER THIRTY-SEVEN

COULD'VE BEEN

"**I** watched that shit," Lil Daye said. Via the FaceTime image, he looked to be in his bedroom in Atlanta wearing a red do-rag. "What's it got to do with me?"

"The man who is paying you and me a ton of money is down with the destruction of black people," D said.

"What I got from the video was that he was trying to make money. I got that. But for him to fuck black people up, we'd have to help him."

"We *are* helping him. He's funneling his money to build private prisons and support white supremacist groups He's doing his best to fuck black people over, and to some degree we are now part of that."

Lil Daye wasn't going to be guilt-tripped. "You're the one who made the introduction. You should have checked this shit out. Now you want me to do something to fuck up this money and my wife's money too? That's some sad-ass managing."

D had known this wasn't going to be easy. He fell back on the talking points he'd prepared. "I'm thinking we can get some of the money we're making funneled to different progressive groups. Really beef up your charity and inoculate—"

"Inoculate?"

D explained: "Protect your brand by aligning you with groups that help black folks and minorities, so if and when this comes out, we can plead innocence."

"How many people know about this tape, D?" Lil Daye's gears were finally moving.

"Not many. Apparently, it just surfaced."

"Then you need to pay all those people off. You need to get that shit shut down."

"That's on Kurtz, don't you think?"

Lil Daye frowned. "I gotta talk this whole thing over with my wife."

"Don't tell Ant," D said. "Promise me that until you make a decision you'll keep him out of it. I feel like he's too in awe of Kurtz. We need to have a clear head about all this."

"Ant started as a pimp," Lil Daye said. This was the first time that info had been passed onto D. It confirmed what he already knew, but it was good to hear Lil Daye admit it. "We all know that. But he wouldn't sell black people out. You don't know him like I do."

"Okay. I trust you to do the right thing. But we need a strategy and we need it soon."

The MC's image disappeared off D's computer screen. D realized that might have been his last conversation with Lil Daye.

CHAPTER THIRTY-EIGHT
RIVER

It all started with a phone call. The producer of the proposed *Accidental Hunter* series called to say his company was not renewing its option on D's life rights. D hadn't been emotionally involved in the project, but when the call ended he still felt a sting. He'd hoped Ray Ray could get a spot on the writing team. Oh well.

Then the offer to send a producer to Paris (maybe Night) to work with a French pop star went away. Apparently, Pharrell was taking the gig. Fair enough. But what followed was a week in which two clients fired D Management and a video game negotiation where D Management clients would have provided music and voice-over work fell apart. D Management's social media accounts were then hacked by posts for erectile dysfunction and MAGA caps.

The biggest blow came when Ant rang from Atlanta.

"I'm calling to tell you that Lil Daye and Mama Daye are firing you. He thanks you for doing an okay job. Now he's moving on."

"Ant, is this because of the video I sent him?"

"It's because he decided to move on, bruh. You can think it's about anything you want. It don't matter to him and it really don't mean shit to me. Just don't be talking about us and we won't be talking about you. We can end like gentlemen or it can get dirty. That's on you. Our attorney will contact you shortly."

"Is Lil Daye gonna call me?"

"Maybe. But that won't change shit."

"So," D said, his anger rising, "I take it that Lil Daye is gonna maintain his relationship with Kurtz despite what that man believes in?"

"Lil Daye is gonna do what's best for him and his people."

"You mean for *you*, don't you? You're pimping Lil Daye like those girls in Atlanta."

"I'm through talking to you. You should mind your business, bruh. If I was you, I'd stay focused on that. What we do and how we do it has nothin' to do with you anymore."

The call was followed by the *Billboard* article, which D thought would be a puff piece, but turned out to be a sour article about D Management losing big-name clients, rumors of financial misdealing, and old-fashioned incompetence. At first, none of these setbacks seemed connected, but they quickly began to feel orchestrated. When Mama Daye tweeted, *You gotta watch who you let in your circle cos everybody ain't ready*, with *#DManagement*, and it got reposted on the pages of many upcoming MCs and singers, D knew something was up.

In a month, it felt like D Management had gone from Motown to Death Row. The next staff meeting was tense.

"We're losing clients," Mal said. "It feels like someone is out to get us."

"Or," D said, "out to get *me*, and you guys are suffering because of it."

"Who would do that? Sounds like a conspiracy theory. Maybe we just aren't doing a good enough job."

"If that's the case, then again, it would be about me," D said. "Maybe I'm in over my head. Still, it feels like someone is def pushing me under." D told his team about Kurtz's true political leanings, his conversation with Lil Daye about the videotape, and the MC firing him, and that he thought Kurtz was behind D Management's current troubles.

Marcy looked around the room at her coworkers and asked, "Shouldn't we go public with what we know about Kurtz?"

D said, "I could. But aren't we in business? We aren't CNN or the *Times*. We could leak it. Someone would air it. It would get all across the Internet. But what do we gain from that? Fox News starts huffing and puffing. People begin trying to trace it back to us. Right now we have a low-level quiet battle going on. If this goes public—I dunno how we win. We should be doing business, not be at war with a major corporation."

"So what's your plan?" It was Ray Ray.

"Let's try to find new business," D replied. "Let's rebuild our roster. Let's talk again to the agencies. We must have some goodwill out there."

Ray Ray said, "That's it?"

"No. But what I will do on offense is not something I'm gonna share right now. When it happens, you'll be the first to know."

Mal said, "Sounds like you don't trust us."

"I trust you all," D responded. "But everything smart isn't done in sunlight."

After the meeting ended, Marcy lingered in D's office. "Are you thinking of closing up the place?" she asked.

"Real talk: I'm thinking I cost us hundreds of thousands of dollars in billing," D said, shaking his head. "The artist I advised didn't care that the guy I got him in business with is a possible Klan member. For Lil Daye, this was never really about hip hop—hip hop was a girl he kissed to get her Daddy's money. He'll toss that woman aside in a heartbeat. I was just a motherfucking tool or, if I'm really talking truth, some bitch he met on the road."

Marcy wasn't impressed. "Nice monologue, D. Like the pimply elements. But you didn't answer my question."

"My answer: not this week."

Marcy said, "That answer sucks."

As the sense that D Management was in trouble grew more public, D received a medley of calls from friends and advisers.

"So," Dr. Funk said, "you must be getting kinda lonely."

D laughed at Dr. Funk's tone, like he was amazed that anyone would leave D alone. "I've def had more sociable moments. How are you doing, my friend?"

"Thanks to you, I'm okay. Just wanted to let you know I ain't leaving you. Against my wishes, you brought me back, and I'm still mad at you, so you gots to stay my manager."

This made D smile. The crazy old man had called to cheer him up and D loved him for it.

"Has anyone called you about leaving my company?"

Dr. Funk whistled. "Ohh boy. Some millennial-type woman called me bad-mouthing you and talking a lot of digital ying-yang. When they decide to move on you, D, it comes from all damn angles."

"You remember her name?"

"Bowman. Strange name for a sista, if you ask me."

Belinda Bowman. The attorney he'd met with Pilgrim. Was he behind this? Felt too obvious, but maybe?

Dr. Funk knew a lot about being ridiculed. He'd gone from pop icon to punch line in the eighties. He'd spent much of the twenty-first century busking on LA street corners and living in the basement of an abandoned building behind a closed nightclub. D had found him, fought Serene Powers over him (taking an L in the process), and had come to love this once-lost genius.

"When I started to have my problems, it seemed like everybody who ever thought I was an asshole got together and made a pact to spread the word. Remember how I was when you met me? That was the end point of a long-ass journey down. I wasn't in my right mind when it started and then that drug thing I got into didn't help. I couldn't stop falling. So, D, you continue working out like you do, eat good, and don't settle for easy pussy."

Next, he heard from R'Kaydia.

"So," D asked her, "what are you hearing?"

"What am I *not* hearing? Word is you're toxic, D. The white boys at the agencies are talking bad about you—bad judgment, in over your head, side deals against your clients' wishes, vague talk of economic malfeasance. You're a black man in Hollywood so it don't take much to ruin your rep. You saw how quick your boy Gibbs went down."

"You talking bad about me too, R'Kaydia? I'd understand if you did. Self-preservation is the LA golden rule."

"It's the rule, whether you call it gold, silver, or platinum. Officially, our business relationship is on pause. That means I'm honoring our existing contracts but initiating no new business."

"Okay."

"But," R'Kaydia said with genuine warmth, "you know we have a special relationship, D. You know that."

"Well, it's good to hear you say that but I don't know much right now. You got a life raft to offer?"

"As you know, Kurtz owns a piece of my company and I consult for DIB. I'm gonna see if I can get some intel on what's going on there. Something you can use."

"Thank you, R'Kaydia."

"How are you for money?"

"I've been poor before. I've been in debt before. But never in a place that's warm. I'll survive. Lots of nightclubs in LA need experienced doormen."

Then Al called.

"Okay, explain this to me again," he said.

"I told my client what I found out," D said, "and he told his man Ant, and I figure they called Kurtz and decided I was trying to get in the way of their money. I could go public. Put the info on the Net or feed it to some aggressive blogger or the *New York Times*. But in the era of Trump, would that bring down Kurtz or make him a Fox News/White House hero? Lil Daye stayed with DIB, I think, because Ant wouldn't let him leave, and I believe Kurtz has Ant in his back pocket. Kindred spirits. Public disclosure would put Lil Daye in a bind and cause a whole shitstorm, and I'm not sure who would get splattered. Did I expect Kurtz would get the entire Hollywood establishment to turn on me? I was naive. So here I am. Call me a fool."

"Fool," Al replied, then laughed.

"Thanks, Al. Just what I needed."

"I'm like LAPD. Protect and serve."

"More like pollute and swerve," D said. "So you've heard me yak. How are you?"

"Your hologram business has seriously augmented my retirement fund. That makes my health good by default. I can offer up some support clichés if you like."

"Feel free."

"It's always darkest before the dawn. There's no place to go but up. A punch in the face is a small sacrifice for victory."

"*Punch in the face*? I've never heard that one."

"I'm older and wiser than you, so I've heard decades more bullshit," Al said, and laughed again.

"I bet. By the way, Al, I love you. Thought I'd toss that your way."

"Feel the same about you, D. Stay up and let me know how I can help."

The WhatsApp connection to Costa Rica was so sharp that D heard birds in the background as Walter Gibbs spoke.

"Nigga, you should just come down here."

"Nawn. I feel like I need to be here and figure this out."

"Ain't nothing to figure out," Gibbs said. "You should have kept that shit to yourself. If it came out, you could have just claimed to be blindsided. That kid wasn't walking away from that bag over principle. All these kids talk *woke*, but they ain't. Come down here. I'll set you up in a spot. You can sit there and talk with the monkeys. Much nicer than the people you know in LA."

"So that's your advice?"

"In that town, the old-white-boy network is deep. They got each others' back, front, and ass. The ones who got MeToo'd are still getting checks. They just took their name off shit, but dollars are still flowing. Don't get that twisted. Now, if I was still up there, maybe I could help, but nigga, I'm in a rain forest every day talking to cockatoos and picking cacao off of trees."

"Well, Gibbs, I'm glad you're happy."

"D, if this had happened fifteen or even ten years ago, I'd have been straight-up suicidal. But I'm at a different point in my life. No matter what they think in LA or New York, the world spins on and most people on the planet don't give a damn what happens there. D, you always wanted to look out for people, but these motherfuckers can't see past their own noses. I know I couldn't."

"You weren't as bad as most, Gibbs."

"I know who I am better than anybody. Anyway, you know Ice is your real problem. Better to be aboveground than under it. He might think 'cause you're vulnerable that to cap your ass is his best move."

"The thought has occurred."

"Just let me know, D," Gibbs said. "The monkeys are waiting."

CHAPTER THIRTY-NINE
FOCUS

There was a moment during vinyasa when D felt his breath elevate him, so that the ache in his left knee, the tension in his lower right buttock, the sweat dripping into his eyes dissipated and he was connected to something beyond himself, the room, and the world.

This elevated feeling didn't last—it was summer-breeze fleeting. Still, it pleased D deeply and he wondered if this was a mild version of samadhi, the elusive moment of transcendence yogis chased eternally.

In shavasana, D lay down but his mind raced. His subconscious unleashed itself. Gigabytes, terabytes, jpegs, MP3s, opinions, dreams, and sorrows flooded him. His subconscious put them in an alignment D could never have consciously created. At the end of most hot yoga classes, D wiped the sweat off his face and gazed around the room, admiring the lithe bodies of women clustered at the front. But today, he didn't see them. He saw photos on a vision board linked by red threads that suggested a way to proceed. D had to take control. He had to use all he'd learned from all the lawyers, agents, and gangstas. Meditation time was over.

D was a situational vegan. He knew it was healthy. He knew many good-looking women loved vegan food. But taste-wise, fake chicken really didn't do much for him. Gracias Madre, which was a vegan Mexican spot with high ceilings and a wide outdoor dining area, was as flavorful as vegan got. At least, that's what D's taste buds had decided. It seemed to be the best place to invite Maggie; they hadn't spoken since he'd left for New York. They'd texted a bit but he'd avoided talking to her, and now he had to, and not for reasons she'd like.

She entered wearing black jeans, black Converse, and a short leather jacket over a Wonder Woman T-shirt. She gave him a short, impersonal hug and then sat down, looking him over like a hanging judge.

"You ghosted me, D."

"I'm sorry, Maggie. I apologize. I've been dealing with a lot of personal and professional demons. Business has been bad. My personal stuff worse. I really needed to deal with them."

"I thought friends relied on friends. But maybe I was wrong. Maybe we aren't real friends yet, 'cause no real friends of mine would have ghosted me like that."

"I know. We had a great connection and I tossed that away. Not consciously. Life got crazy."

"Okay," Maggie said, softening. "What's up with you now?"

"I'm working on getting my life back together, and I need your help to do it."

"Really? After leaving me standing and looking like a fool at that Nas show, you want to ask me a favor?"

"Yes. It's about Kurtz." D related a truncated version of Robinson's book, Lil Daye's reaction, and the potential danger he was in.

Maggie didn't ask any questions and looked seriously uncomfortable. "Kurtz," she said slowly, "is a nasty man to have on your ass. I like you, D, but if you invited me here to help you do something against Kurtz, I'm not sure if I can or even want to."

D never thought he had much game when it came to women, but he knew he'd need to summon what little he had to get Maggie to aid him. "All I need from you are the names of two girls who may have made deposits on Kurtz's toy room. In fact, no need for real names. Just gimme their Instagram handles. That's all."

Maggie shook her head and looked away before responding. "I'll need more than vegan Mexican and some chickpeas to do that for you."

"What do you use? PayPal? Venmo?"

"Venmo. Are you really gonna pay me?"

"Five Gs for two Instagram addresses. Sound good?"

"Seven," she shot back.

"So how about now we go dutch for dinner?"

"Funny boy," she said. "But I don't need your money, D, and I'm insulted you even suggested it. I was just joking. But I see you think I'm about money."

"If I offended you, I'm so sorry. I apologize."

"If you think you're better than Kurtz, don't. He offered me money too. Actually, it was a car."

"Money for—"

"Information on you."

It turned out that Kurtz (or people who worked for him) had been monitoring her social media and had seen images of them together. He'd offered her a sports car if she'd give him updates on D's movements, things he talked about, and details on who he was meeting with.

"Shit," D said.

"But you're good. I turned him down. Not that I really owe you any loyalty, but that man is creepy. Creepier than you know."

"Please tell me whatever you can."

Ten minutes, two mojitos, and dual action on their respective smartphones later, Maggie said, "Take a look at your Instagram."

Flame23 and FitFranny were different ethnicities—Flame was Japanese and Franny was Jamaican—but both shared the same toned shoulders, six-pack abs, doll-like smiles, and long raven hair.

"I won't use your name, Maggie," he assured her. "In fact, I won't be the one contacting them. So don't worry about being connected."

"D, you know good and well there's something to worry about. I'll tell you why: he owns a brothel."

Maggie gave him the address, which D googled. A posh residence with gates surrounding it on a beautiful street in Beverly Hills.

"How do you know about this?"

"I know," she said firmly, and sipped on her third mojito.

D decided not to push her further. She was already telling him a lot. He didn't feel he knew her well enough to keep probing. He liked Maggie a great deal but knew that with this conversation, they were closing the doors between them.

"If you're gonna take Kurtz down, then take him down for the right reasons. Not just for your ego or whatever business war you have with him. Hurting him will help friends of mine. That's why I'ma help you."

"Okay," D said. "Now let's have some more mojitos."

CHAPTER FORTY

TILL IT'S DONE

D sat looking at highlights of the 1994 NBA Finals, trying to will in a couple more of John Starks's jump shots in game seven. No luck. The Knicks would lose again, a bitter memory from D's past that he revisited occasionally like he was taking revenge on himself.

Two calls were about to come in that would alter his mood. The first was from Marcy Mui. Word was that her résumé was floating around town and it was only a matter of time before he'd receive her resignation from D Management. D looked at the name on his screen and wondered if this was a goodbye call.

"I have something to tell you, D," she said.

"If you have a great offer, you have to do what's right for you," he replied.

"What? I'm not leaving, D. But I did just get offered a job. I turned it down, but that's why I'm calling you. It was from the attorney Belinda Bowman."

D was surprised. "To join her law firm?"

"Her new management company."

"Whoa," he said. "That kinda makes sense with all the calls she's been making."

"She's signed Lil Daye."

"What?!"

"There's more: apparently Amos Pilgrim is backing her company. He's a silent partner."

"Hmmm. He's her mentor. With his backing and her hustle, they might have something."

"I thought you were tight with him," Marcy said.

"We know each other well, but *tight*? We ain't tight."

D was wondering if he could find a YouTube clip of some other horrible New York sports moment when Serene's name popped up on his smartphone. *Be good to me*, D prayed.

"Come meet me, D. Out by the pier in Santa Monica."

D frowned. "I'm not big on the ocean right now, Serene. I guess we could play skittle ball at the arcade."

He could almost hear Serene shaking her head. "I'm not inviting you to play games," she said. "I have the help you asked for, so get your ass out here."

Forty minutes later, D and Serene walked down the crowded pier, passing the mostly Mexican American and Asian families that strolled slowly and crowded around food and souvenir stands that leaned against the metal fences that separated folks from the Pacific Ocean.

"How are you?"

"Considering bodyguard work," he said with a tight smile. "If not, there's always working the door at the Hotel Café."

"I don't think that'll be necessary," Serene said, "if you do what's *really* necessary. That's why I called you. I thought you'd be interested once I passed on this info."

At the end of Santa Monica Pier, tourists took selfies and photographed sea lions. Buskers covered pop hits with guitars and miniature drum machines. Two sets of hard gray steps faced out toward the Pacific. Sitting on the steps closest to Venice Beach was a small light-skinned woman wearing a black beret, slacks, jacket, and boots. She was petite with a fierce light in her eyes. She spoke with an accent D didn't recognize.

"I have information for you, Mr. Hunter," she began. "It's about a very naughty man named Samuel Kurtz." She reached into her coat and handed D a manila envelope. "I can provide you with digital copies later, when I have a secure link ready. I thought this would suffice for now."

The papers and photos bore *Interpol* stamps and detailed Kurtz's activities as a client partner in several human-trafficking networks that brought women from Africa to Spain and Italy. On business trips, he'd visited brothels in Madrid and Milan to inspect his "merchandise," a.k.a. poor African women in search of European employment.

D eyed the small woman with suspicion. "Do you work for Interpol?"

She smiled. "We have a relationship with certain elements of that organization."

Serene cut in: "Helen and her team are not law enforcement. They have a different mission. They repatriate African art from European museums. I helped them when I was in Europe and they agreed to help me and, in the process, you."

"I know you are doing Serene a favor," D said, "but you have no reason to help *me*."

"We support what Serene does for women, and since Kurtz is an exploiter of African women, it makes sense to help you. But one day we might send you a bill."

"Figured as much," D grumbled. "Just for the record: I'm not a thief, Helen."

"No thieves here," she said. "We're Liberators, Mr. Hunter."

* * *

The stuff they'd given him on Kurtz was fire. Just what he'd hoped for. But these Liberators? He was now in debt to a bunch of Afrocentric zealots who robbed European museums and galleries of dusty masks and rusty statues. He figured that one day this could be a problem. But right now there were more moves to make.

CHAPTER FORTY-ONE
ANOTHER LIFE

The T-shirts on the shelf were variations of the same slogan. One read, *Don't be self-conscious. Embrace subconscious.* Another read, *Don't be self-conscious. Be subconscious.* The most popular read, *Fuck self-consciousness. Love subconscious.* D smiled, then handed the blissed-out blonde behind the counter his credit card for admittance to a talk by the tees' creator.

This afternoon, Melanie Drift was appearing at an upscale yoga studio in Pacific Palisades. A variety of products (the tees, a self-published book, a line of scented candles, bracelets, necklaces, etc.) were being hawked alongside the studio's yoga mats and pants, Sanskrit translations, and prayer beads.

"The healing path can be such an amazing roller-coaster ride," she said in an even, soothing tone that felt like hands caressing your face. "Healing and the evolution of consciousness are rarely what or how we think they will be. There is nothing that you need to be afraid of or doubt yourself about. It is all learning and it is all on the healing path. Set and keep your intention. Everything and everyone that comes into your life is there to support your healing and evolution and vice versa. Everything is for your benefit and for the benefit of all when we let go, and remember that it's always working out when we allow it.

"When I work on myself and my clients, it's so key to allow the healing energy, emotions, pain, and thoughts to move through. It can be fun, painful, scary, and blissful, but it doesn't need to make sense to work and do its job."

After Melanie signed books, hugged followers, and spoke warmly to people seeking instruction, she gestured for D to follow her into an empty yoga studio. When D entered, she closed the door behind him and looked him over with a critical eye.

Using his most charming voice, D said, "Thank you for meeting with me, Melanie."

This didn't impress the spiritual instructor. "You are here because I respect Serene Powers and the work she does. I have no real interest in you and not much respect for the kind of culture you promote. Just so we're clear."

"Okay," he said. "You've read the testimonies we've collected about Kurtz's activities with women—both professionally and at his place in Malibu. Will you help?"

"We'll see," she replied coolly. "Before I make my decision, I just wanted to see you face-to-face. I wasn't sure if you were a real victim or just a common blackmailer."

"Isn't this really about who he is?" D said, not backing down.

"Serene told me your story. You've had a lot of tragedy in your life. But you know whatever your pain, it doesn't justify inflicting injury on others. What you want me to do will hurt more than your target. It will hurt his wife, his children, and people you'll never know." She was scolding D and he had to take it.

"If you're asking if I want revenge, I'd have to say I want justice," he said softly. "That's how I see it. Not just for me but for the people he exploits."

"He is a destructive force. I know that. I just needed to get a better sense of why you want to destroy him. I have that now."

"Well then, I leave it to you."

"Mr. Hunter, don't ever mention this conversation and never attend any of my events again."

"Okay. Can you tell me your decision then?"

"You'll know my decision by being present in the world."

No goodbye. Melanie just opened the studio door and left. D didn't know what she would do. All he was certain of was that Kurtz's wife Sylvia was one of the women Melanie consulted via video chat every Tuesday at two p.m., Pacific time. Melanie had a direct connection to the consciousness of a woman who could do serious damage to Kurtz's life. At least that's what Serene felt when she'd set up this meeting. But would Melanie Drift share the damaging information about Kurtz with his wife? If so, would that information push her to divorce her husband? D knew it was dirty. But if he was going to damage Kurtz, he was going to use every tool he could.

On his way out of the yoga studio, D saw Maggie enter with a fit sandy-haired white man. She wore white Birkenstocks, formfitting white yoga pants, and an athletic bra. She looked ready to sweat, open her root chakra, and have great tantric sex. The man with her had a well-groomed Maroon 5 beard and the cocky carriage of a former college quarterback. It was a lovely multiracial vision of Cali love that D wanted to avoid. He turned his back and stuck his head into one of Melanie's books until he heard Maggie's voice disappear down the hallway.

D walked out of the yoga studio into the glare of the California sun.

CHAPTER FORTY-TWO
THE CHARADE

"**B**een a crazy weekend, hasn't it?" Pilgrim said, referencing the Trump-driven headlines on the newspapers spread before him on the table. The *Wall Street Journal*, the *New York Times*, the *Los Angeles Times*, the *Daily News*, an iPad, and two cell phones were all scattered on the table—most them featuring images from or headlines about the weekend's white riot in Charlottesville, Virginia. "All this Trump mess and the crazy people it has inspired."

D sat down and replied, "This one would def go on the hard side of the ledger."

"I love you that you said *ledger*, D," Pilgrim said, suddenly a little lighter. "No one who works for me now has a clue what a ledger book is. If it isn't on a phone or in a digital file, it means nothing to them. Most of my staff barely know how to hold a pen, much less use one. I don't know if any of the people I pay could write their own signature if their life depended on it."

D noticed that Pilgrim was looking a little healthier. He seemed refreshed, like he'd just come back from a spa weekend with a new liver and freshly scrubbed skin. His eyes were clear and his skin shone. Had it been another day, maybe D would have asked about his "wellness" regime. But D wasn't in the mood to give the old man compliments. "I'm not feeling very philosophical, Amos. Sorry."

"People aren't very observant anymore. If it isn't on a screen, it makes no impact. As you see, I love newspapers. But these screens—damned if they aren't useful."

D reached into the backpack on the seat next to him and pulled out two clear plastic folders. The top of one read, *Samuel Kurtz*. The other, *Amos Pilgrim*.

Pilgrim looked at both folders like they would electrocute him.

D said, "The material on Kurtz relates to his sexual activities at his Malibu home. It also details his involvement with human trafficking in Europe. You wanna know about your file?"

Pilgrim folded his arms across his chest. "I read slow."

"In that folder are sections of *The Plot Against Hip Hop* that mention you," D said, "but not how Dwayne Robinson depicted you. I had it revised by a writer who works for me named Ray Ray."

"So this Ray Ray knows what was there originally?"

"He does," D said, "but he's loyal to me."

"Somehow that doesn't make me all that comfortable."

"Well *I'm* comfortable," D said. "You need to be focused to do something good with that information on Kurtz."

"All right. First of all, no need to go public with this," Pilgrim said. "Maybe eventually we'll do a leak here or there. But there's another way to go. A way to break Kurtz's heart."

"What's that?"

"I'm on the board of DIB. Over the next few weeks, watch your screens. Just watch your screens."

"That's vague, but okay, I'm trusting you, Amos. I'll have the altered book ready in case I have to share it, and I'll send you the video of Kurtz. I'm gonna give you a shot at doing the right thing."

"A wise move," Pilgrim said. "Don't do anything else, D. I will handle it."

"So, I take it you were the other party investigating Kurtz?"

"Now that we are truly partners in crime, I guess it's all right to say yes."

"I got some pressure on me, Amos. Some stuff you hopefully know nothing about. Unless you do."

"I don't know what you're talking about." The old man tried to look innocent but wasn't very convincing.

"All right, tell me about Belinda Bowman. Is she working for Kurtz?"

"I believe so. I introduced them. He thought she was bright and could be useful. Plus he likes 'ethnic' women. But don't blame her. She's trying to get ahead just like you are."

D shook his head and sighed. "So is Ben Carson, and look how well that's gone."

CHAPTER FORTY-THREE

HOW MUCH
A DOLLAR COST

"**I**'m gonna get a place in Marina del Rey, pardner," Ant said between sips on his Sinsere with cranberry juice. "Get me a condo overlooking the ocean. Gonna get my office set up in Santa Monica over by where Amazon and HBO is. Universal Music is over in that complex too. They offered me a deal but all we need from them is distribution. Gonna get a Cash Money type of deal. Been talking with Birdman. But Lil Daye is already bigger than Lil Wayne ever got, so he can only tell me so much."

Ice looked over Ant's shoulder at two Kim Kardashian clones with fake eyelashes and bone-straight hair who took selfies while batting their eyes. Sitting before them was a healthy bowl of broccoli and salmon, which they ignored in favor of self-promotion. Ice, Ant, and the ladies doing selfies sat on the patio of Tocaya Organica on Sunset Boulevard. Ice brought his gaze back to Ant's lumpy body and smiled thinly. Wish fulfillment was a motherfucker.

At Ice's request, Ant had given him a printed report on everything he knew about D Hunter's LA activities (addresses, e-mails, habits), so there was no electronic footprint. The report sat on the table next to the bowl of chicken tinga, brown rice, and avocado that Ice was eating. Ant continued rambling about how he was going to conquer Hollywood and that Lil Daye was just the first step in his plan for media domination. He hinted at "serious connections" in Los Angeles. Ant's self-hype bored Ice, but he was in LA to do a job, so he listened, nodding occasionally while he kept an eye on people entering the restaurant.

Ice had been unsure how he was going to find out who'd hired him when he arrived in LA via a five-day Amtrak ride across America. Flying was out of the question and he didn't feel like driving—too many small-town cops, too many speed traps. But when he arrived in his motel on Crenshaw, Pablo had, of all things, faxed Ice a sheet with the phone numbers of the man who'd called him. Pablo and his family were, as Ice had suggested, in the wind. Pablo's parting gesture of loyalty had been unearthing one last identity.

Turned out the overweight boaster sitting across from Ice was the contractor, though. Ice didn't buy that this guy was paying the bills. Hood guys like this usually paid gangbangers to do this work 'cause they were making street-level moves on other street-level players. Ant wouldn't have had the patience to track Ice down, contact Pablo, and then wire that money. Ant, Ice thought, was a stack-of-hundreds-in-a-paperback kind of dude. Someone was working him.

"So when I get situated out here, I'ma need a team of hitters," Ant said. "I got a crew coming in from ATL, but none of them have your pedigree, Ice. I think—"

"Yo, we got lucky today." Ice's eyes grew as big as saucers. "Look who's at the counter ordering."

Ant turned around and spied D Hunter. "Shit," he said.

"Just sit tight," Ice said. "You a rider, right?"

"Whatchu mean?"

"You know what the fuck I mean."

"You ain't thinking about doing nothing now, are you? Out here on Sunset?"

"You want it done, right? Well, now you can be part of it. Don't be scared."

"I ain't scared."

"Okay, boss. Wait here."

Ant wanted to turn around but kept his eyes focused on his guacamole and chips. Blood rushed through his body. His saliva grew bitter with bile. Finally, he couldn't take it any longer and turned around. No D. No Ice. Just girls taking selfies in the Cali sun. He received a text: *Come to the parking lot.*

The lot ran along a slope behind a row of boutiques and bistros. Ant found Ice standing with arms folded next to Ant's blue Tesla. "Look in the back," Ice said.

On the backseat floor he saw D Hunter, handcuffed and duct-taped. "What the fuck!" Ant shouted.

"Lower your voice, homeslice."

"What's he doing in my car?!"

"Lower your voice and get in," Ice said evenly.

"Get in?"

Ice went to Ant's passenger door and got in. Ant was dumbstruck. This was not what he had in mind. He pulled out his cell. There was a tapping sound on the driver's-side window. There was a 9mm Glock aimed at Ant.

The window rolled down and Ice said, "Get in, boss."

Ant looked down at D and shuddered. "Nigga, I'm not comfortable with this. And how'd you get in my car?"

"Head east, boss," Ice instructed. "I got a spot picked out to dump the body."

Ant's Tesla made a right onto the Sunset Boulevard traffic crawl. Ant was shook. His mind was racing. "He ain't dead, is he?"

"Good as," Ice said.

"You knew he was coming?"

"I did," Ice said, sounding eerily relaxed. "That's why I'm me. Put some music on. Not that mumble-rap either. Some real gangsta shit."

Dr. Dre's *The Chronic* flowed through the speakers as Ant's Tesla rolled along Hollywood, turning left on Gower, up to Franklin, and going east on Los Feliz Boulevard to Griffith Park.

Ant was sweating. He was rubbing his forehead with the back of his hand. "Okay," he said, "what's your plan?"

Ice smiled. "I got somebody meeting me here who'll take care of the body."

"Damn, you really did know he was coming?"

"Just keep going straight," Ice said, "and park next to that white van up ahead."

Once inside Griffith Park, they drove up a long road that emptied into a sparsely populated parking lot. A white van was situated at the far end. When the Tesla pulled up, the van's passenger door opened and a tall, fit woman in a leather jacket, black jeans, and Nike sneakers stepped out. She wore a Donald Trump clown mask adorned with bright orange hair. Despite his anxiety, Ant was fascinated by the way this woman moved. He rolled down his window and said, "Got your package right here, Mr. President."

The Trump mask–wearing woman said, "Yes you do," and stuck a Taser against Ant's neck. He lit up like a fat brown Christmas tree.

When Ant came to, he was tied up in the rear of the white van, lying on his back, looking up at Trump typing on a smartphone. His mouth was gagged or else he would have cursed her out.

"Anthony," the Trump woman said, "you are a human trafficker, a pimp, and a kidnapper. I'm not the law so you won't need an attorney, but you do need a friend. Unfortunately, I'm not your friend. I am going to ask you a series of questions about your activities in Atlanta, what you planned to do in LA—not your show-biz shit but your real work—and your relationship with Samuel Kurtz. I don't expect you to cooperate immediately. In fact, I hope you don't."

She moved up to the front of the van, where a large man sat behind the wheel. Ride was an old associate of D's from Brooklyn who D had helped out of a serious jam involving missing money and a wayward woman. Ride wasn't afraid to get dirty, but he knew that with this woman around, he was just a driver.

"This won't take long," she told Ride. "He's a punk. There's a girl named Dorita who I need to find. He's gonna help me."

"If you're doing the asking," Ride responded, "no question."

CHAPTER FORTY-FOUR

THESE WALLS

Morning light entered through cracks around the covered basement windows. The distant rumble of a truck could be heard. From someone's car stereo, a seventies funk track filtered down into the dusty room. There were some old keyboards, an ancient 808 drum machine, and an equally vintage mixing board in a corner. This had once been a space for creativity and obsession. It had been Dr. Funk's studio and place of exile for a decade. Thankfully, he'd finally moved on.

But the night before, in this spot, a nasty bit of business had been conducted. The floor was moist with spilled water, which was collecting in puddles where the ground was uneven. Two large, empty water bottles rested against a wall. A rat made an appearance, looked around, and decided there was nothing here for him. Serene sighed and then nodded to the huge man standing with his arms folded in the shadows. "We're through here," she said. "You can go. Thank you."

Ride said, "Anything for you, sexy. Let me know when you wanna leave that cook in SF. I'm ready." His smile was almost bashful. Then he came over and hugged Serene, squeezing a little too hard before letting go. "You sure you don't need any help with this?" He gestured over to Ant tied to a metal chair.

Serene shook her head, patted the big man affectionately on his chest, and watched him exit up the staircase. A splash of sunlight filled the basement, illuminating Ant's unconscious, wet body. Then the room was dark again.

Ant's clothes were drenched and his mouth bloody. He'd shit and pissed too, so he stank. Serene knew this kind of interrogation was imperfect, but she needed answers fast. Unfortunately, she hadn't learned everything she wanted to. No, Lil Daye wasn't involved with Ant's illicit sex business. Yes, he'd been brought in by Sam Kurtz to hire Ice and put a hit on D. Yes, he'd pressured Lil Daye into staying attached to DIB at Kurtz's instruction.

Most important to Serene, no, he didn't know where Dorita was now. Serene had asked a number of times in several unpleasant ways. Ant's story was that they'd sold her to some people from NOLA and that she had probably been transported by some dudes he knew to Louisiana. Ant protested that he was just protecting his friend from a blackmailer. That didn't justify shit to Serene. But after an ugly night, she believed she'd gotten everything she could out of Ant. So she emptied the last of the water barrels into a sink and left the drenched Ant tied to the chair.

It was midday in LA. The morning haze had burned away and the sun hung over the city high and hot. Serene went over to the white van and pulled out a yoga mat that she placed on a patch of grass. She removed her dark wet top and bared her upper body to the daylight. Stretching her muscles, Serene went into child's pose and breathed deeply. She got up and did a warrior pose, which felt particularly liberating since it pumped blood into her legs and opened her chest. She felt alive again after the night with Ant.

Inside the van, she put on a yellow and light-blue sundress and sandals, transforming from an avenger to a lady ready for mimosas and brunch. Unfortunately, there was still some necessary housekeeping.

"He passed her on to some crew from New Orleans who moved her down there," she said into her phone. "I believe him."

"Fine," Mildred Barnes said, quite pissy. "You wasted our time on a project that will yield you little useful intel."

"Helping D was something I needed to do," she spat back.

She got no sympathy from Mildred. "I have chosen individuals for you that help to maximize our resources by targeting major human-trafficking networks. That's what I employ you to do. But you run off on personal projects that have nothing to do with our larger mission. I did not recruit you so you could pick up every low-level pimp you encountered, whether it be in London or LA. As distasteful as these people are, this man today was not a big fish and you burned one of our safe houses in the process."

"You ready to take a breath?" Serene asked. "Okay. I'm gonna leave this fool here. I assume you can handle cleaning this up and moving him out. I think maybe I need to take a break. I'll call you when I'm ready to come back. Okay?" It wasn't really a question. She just clicked off.

She and Mildred Barnes shared the same goal, but Serene was no puppet and Mildred increasingly sought control of her actions. Her boyfriend deserved her time and attention. Her MMA career deserved more focus. More work with the Liberators would be fun.

Serene walked away from the van and Dr. Funk's studio out onto Crenshaw Boulevard. It was one of the city's historic streets and the longtime heartbeat of the African American community. She stood in front of what had once been the Heaven's Gate, a club owned by D's grandfather Daniel. That had been a different LA. The city and Crenshaw's black community were shrinking by the day. A sign on the old music venue read, *Future Home of CVS*.

I wonder if D knows about this, she thought.

There was a Starbucks nearby. Once she'd downed some caffeine, she'd call D Hunter. Just a few more things to do before she left town.

CHAPTER FORTY-FIVE
COME DOWN

Samuel Kurtz stood on his deck overlooking the Pacific Ocean and sipped on Sinsere laced with gin. It had become his favorite drink. The sales of Sinsere had been climbing steadily throughout the summer and fall. Hip hop hadn't failed him. It truly moved product like few other advertising platforms.

Other than that, life had lately been a jumble of bad news. His wife had filed for divorce, citing irreconcilable differences. After one teary-eyed call, she refused to speak to him, calling him a monster and suggesting he was a human trafficker. So far, his team had managed to keep the filing out of the public eye, but it could turn ugly.

Unfortunately, some DIB board of directors members had gotten wind of it; after having total control of the members for decades, there was a mutiny brewing. Kurtz had enlisted his friend, and board member, Amos Pilgrim to calm the restless. Pilgrim had suggested bringing on some new members, maybe a woman, to present a progressive female-empowering face to the world. That would be important if the divorce hit the Internet.

Kurtz sensed that someone was orchestrating his difficulties. But who? The president had suggested it was a Democratic/FBI/Comey plot driven by the same forces behind Mueller's unending, un-American Russian probe.

Kurtz had his own FBI sources and that theory seemed like fake news. Not a sentiment he shared with #45 since contradictory facts just made his friend red-faced.

He'd get a handle on everything. He always did. He had the resources. He had the money. He had the power. He'd get his wife back. He'd get the board under control. He had friends and his friends had friends. He'd sort it all out or they would. That's how it always worked.

All that pettiness could be ignored tonight. It was a party night, the biggest he'd enjoyed in Malibu in years. He needed cheering up, and lots of nubile young women were the right medicine. *#MeToo be damned*, he thought. *I can make dreams come true.* Whether you paid for a fuck or dinner or a condo, whether you got married or not, sex was always transactional. As long as he could do things for women, they came running. That was just human nature. It was primal and would never change.

Kurtz was determined to have Maggie tonight. That long-legged mixed chick who had been acting so special, so removed, so above it all, was going to bend to his will. It was time for her to play *his* game. She'd more or less agreed to it on the phone. Not only that, she was bringing a friend.

Kurtz was sitting at the head of his dining table chatting with a movie executive when Maggie and another woman entered. Maggie was, as always, luminous, but her friend stopped Kurtz short. Black latex catsuit, open-toed ankle boots, and hair slicked back in a Sade-like ponytail. She was brown and tall and walked with a runway stride. Kurtz swooned. After all that time waiting on Maggie, he could hardly see her now.

The young woman said, "My name is Dorita," which Kurtz found a disappointing name for a regal presence. He had the dinner table seating changed, moving the Hollywood executive so that Maggie and Dorita sat on either side. Dorita's life story proved intriguing: she was a stylist for celebrity shoots in Paris, London, New York, you name it. More enticing was that Maggie had apparently prepped her regarding Kurtz's unique taste in "entertainment," and she seemed remarkably enthusiastic about an encounter. Kurtz watched her eat a meal of lentils, broccoli, and brown rice, which would make his particular pleasure especially pungent.

After dessert, Kurtz stood by the window, watching the purple, blue, and burgundy sky fade over the Pacific with a couple of male dinner guests when Maggie sauntered over, whispering, "My friend would like to see you privately, if that's all right." Kurtz turned and saw Dorita, her neck and chest bare to him as a virgin to a vampire. Maggie was a meal for another night.

Kurtz took Dorita's hand, guiding her out of the dining room, upstairs, and down the long hallway to his playroom. The air smelled of lavender. The ocean crashed against the shore below. The room's lights were blue as a Miles Davis solo. Kurtz turned toward Dorita and leered. Dorita punched him in the jaw.

Kurtz found himself handcuffed spread-eagle on his bed under his plexiglass playpen. He could have lived with this except that Dorita was not high above him on the plexiglass.

Dorita was squatting right over him with her catsuit off and her body naked. Her smartphone was mounted on a tripod next to the bed. Kurtz tried to scream for security but a pillowcase was jammed in his mouth.

"You don't know who the real Dorita is," the woman said. "I haven't been able to find her. So until I do, let this be a reminder: your shit stinks."

Kurtz had no idea what she was talking about, which made this even crazier. As he kicked and tugged at his restraints, Dorita (a.k.a. Serene Powers) released her bowels on Kurtz's belly, chest, and face. He squirmed and thrashed and flailed, but this rich man was powerless to prevent this digitally recorded humiliation.

Afterward, Serene cleaned herself off in the bathroom and then slid her tripod and camera into a purse.

"Thank you for your time," she said, smirking. "You'll hear from me."

Back downstairs, Serene clinked glasses with Maggie as they shared champagne and then strolled out into the Malibu night toward their waiting town car. They watched the video and laughed loudly before uploading the footage to D Hunter.

He texted right back, *Thanks for this.*

Then Serene directed the driver to LAX. Time to go home.

CHAPTER FORTY-SIX

FOR SALE? (INTERLUDE)

The text was from a number D didn't recognize. In it was a link and the words, *This will be of interest.* D didn't click on the link. It was likely spam. He was about to erase it when a text from R'Kaydia popped up. It read, *Good news,* and had the same link.

It was a press release from DIB corporate communications.

Samuel L. Kurtz is stepping down as CEO and chairman of Diversified International Brands effective immediately. Board members Richard R. Antioch and Amos H. Pilgrim will assume the mantle of cochairs in the interim period until a new permanent chairman is installed. R'Kaydia Lelilia Jenkins, owner of Future Life Communications and an innovator in performance content delivery, has joined the board to fill the gap created by Kurtz's exit.

Whoa!

He'd hoped to hear that Kurtz was out, but Amos as cochairman and R'Kaydia on the board was a crazy twist. D called the number of the unknown texter and a female voice answered.

"Mr. Hunter, so good to hear from you. My name is Catherine Anderson. I'm a special assistant to Chairman Amos Pilgrim of DIB. He would love to schedule a meeting with you for later this week. How is Thursday morning at—"

"The Four Seasons."

"Yes. Shall we say eight thirty a.m.?"

When D arrived, R'Kaydia was sipping tea and tapping on her iPad at Amos Pilgrim's usual table. After sharing a polite hug, D sat down and glanced around the room for the waiter/MC, but he wasn't on the floor.

D said solemnly, "It's not like Amos to be late."

"Well," R'Kaydia said, "Amos had been planning his retirement. Now he's the chairman of a multinational global beverage enterprise and fielding calls from around the world from very concerned stockholders, suppliers, and executives. Turns out Kurtz wasn't very popular, but no one likes instability. He'll be here soon but I can brief you on his offer."

"Wow," D said, very amused, "you will make a fine corporate executive."

Her voice became a harsh whisper: "I don't know what you did, D. I probably don't want to know."

"You don't."

"But DIB is going to offer you a consulting gig. Probably worth several hundred thousand to you personally and a lot more to your management company. Amos knows you got messed up by Lil Daye and his crew. Kurtz too, I'm sure. I have to admit, it's worked out well for me."

"I'm thankful for that," D said. "You are breaking the glass ceiling with this, R'Kay."

"Which is why I was probably a little tight when you walked up. I have this feeling—I know it's a true feeling—that lots of people are watching me now."

"They are. They definitely are. You'll be fine. Now, I'm gonna go."

R'Kaydia didn't know what to make of this. "I'm sure Amos will be along shortly. You know he never misses breakfast here, D."

"I know," D said, deadly serious, "but I'm gonna go in a minute. I want you to give him this message: *I know you used me*. It took me awhile to figure it out. It was Amos who got Conrad to look into Mayer's murder as a way to draw me out. He'd had Dwayne Robinson's manuscript the whole time. He got me to move on Kurtz. If Kurtz got to me first, he'd have gotten me out of the way. I'd never be a threat to him again. I'm not sure if he was behind Gibbs getting hit with MeToo charges, but didn't he advise you to reach out to me about partnering up?"

"Yes. But I would have wanted to anyway. D, this train of thought is crazy."

"I don't think so. He knew about Ice and hired him to kill me."

The usually composed R'Kaydia looked wide-eyed at D. "Do you know how insane you sound right now?"

"Not insane, R'Kaydia," he said sadly. "Just got my eyes open and my mind right. I helped Amos pull down Kurtz for him. Helped you get on the board. I'm happy for you, really. But I'm not through with Amos. Tell him that."

R'Kaydia was bewildered as D walked out of the Four Seasons. She had no idea what he was talking about. Before she called Amos, she needed to do some research of her own.

CHAPTER FORTY-SEVEN
MARCY ME

D got a massage at a Chinese spot in Sunset Plaza that Maggie had recommended, but the ninety-minute session hadn't stilled his anxiety. It would take more than a small Chinese woman's firm hands to remove all the tension embedded in his muscles. With his mind swirling, D decided to walk home, passing the Standard Hotel (which had once been his early '00s home away from home), and the DGA building, then made a right on Fairfax heading south. Until you hit Melrose, where there was a high school and hip street-fashion district, Fairfax wasn't architecturally interesting. This was perfect for D. He could zone out as he walked, since the street was the blankest of slates.

Crossing Santa Monica, Fairfax sloped downhill into bland obscurity—buildings and businesses no one looked twice at. D was doing his walking meditation when he felt a presence from his past. He knew not to make any sudden moves. Out on the street was a blue Audi slowly cruising a few steps behind him. The passenger-side window rolled down. The smooth-faced man behind the wheel asked, "You know a good place for lunch?"

Twenty minutes later, Ice was raving about the chicken tikka masala, particularly the sauce, which he was happily scooping up. D knew they had to meet, but the hit man's unexpected presence had him shook—even as Ice gleefully took a spoonful of D's lentils.

"This is a good hookup, D. Thought you'd have me eating at a strictly vegan place."

Badmaash on Fairfax had become D's local hangout, a place that balanced excellent Indian with an all–hip hop playlist. The staff was friendly, so they'd remember who D was with if his body was found bound and gagged in Pan Pacific Park tomorrow. Jay-Z's "Marcy Me" filled the restaurant. Ice sat back in his chair. "Damn good food," he said, "and damn good Jay. No wonder you like it here."

Ice had shaved his beard and head, now looking like a twenty-pounds-lighter Ving Rhames. His diamond earring was back. This was the face of Brownsville Ice, though his retiree movements remained. He'd lost his disguise but not the loose normalcy that had given his disguise credibility. On close inspection, Ice was either in transition from normalcy back to crime, or stuck like overlapping reflections in a funhouse mirror.

They hadn't spoken much after Serene stuffed Ant in that van. Ice and D had taken separate cars, parked in different lots, and left at different times. D had been carrying an envelope on him ever since, not knowing when or where Ice would appear. Now he unzipped his backpack and passed over the payment.

"Gracias," Ice said with a smile. "So do you know who was behind that clown Ant?"

"I spoke to Serene."

"That bad bitch? Whoa, I know she got the answer out of dude."

"I don't want to tell you. I'll handle it myself," D said.

"What's that mean? I know you ain't puttin' in work at this late date."

"I don't want to have any more bodies haunting me, Ice. You can understand that."

"I can, but I won't," Ice said with his head lowered, his eyes slits. "That motherfucker kind of scared me, D. Made me insecure. I'm too old to be insecure. I got their money but I want their head. You need to give me a name."

"Not head. *Heads*. Based on what Serene got from Ant and what I've figured out, Kurtz and Pilgrim both hired you, then later had a falling-out. Pilgrim flipped on Kurtz, blackmailing him with the help of another friend of mine. Point is, I want to handle this in a legal and open way."

Ice didn't seem to find this very convincing. "Okay, but will 'legal' really protect you? These motherfuckers have money and power. I'm not the only man in these United States who does what I do."

"Gimme a window to do things my way. If I need you, I'll reach out. If something happens to me, well, you'd be on your own."

"Okay," Ice said, then smiled. "I will fall back. But only on one condition: I would love to pursue an acting career."

"Ice, c'mon."

"I know," he said almost innocently. "My face can't appear on-screen. But I got stories to tell. Lots of stories. Whether it's a documentary or episodic TV. Half the shit on Netflix is about crime. Manage me, D, as a storyteller. That way I can pursue my dream and watch your back."

"You are buggin', Ice," D responded with a laugh. "You are really buggin'. But you know what? It makes sense. I have a young writer—a kid from Brownsville—who I can connect you with."

"So," Ice said, reaching a hand across the table, "we got a deal?"

CHAPTER FORTY-EIGHT

BACK TO THE FUTURE
(PART I)

After the unexpected meeting with Ice, D walked back to his place at the Palazzo West. He went out on his balcony overlooking 3rd Street. In his hands was Dwayne Robinson's manuscript, a Cohiba cigar, and a lighter. He fired up his cigar and looked over at the Grove outdoor mall across the street.

If he burned the manuscript, D could break a cycle. He would finally be released from the past that the manuscript represented, freeing himself to fully live a swanky LA life. These pages were a link to his years as a bodyguard; this old stuff from a dead man's book. No one would miss it. Strike a match and all that history becomes ash. Not to be forgotten was the possibility that the distribution of this manuscript could lead the NYPD to reopen the cold Mayer case and lead them to go reinterview Jackson/Jones in jail.

A gust of wind hit D's cigar. The burning dulled. The smoke faded. He tried to relight it, but the wind kept blowing. So he just kept the cigar stuck in his mouth and gently chewed on the moist tobacco. *Fires do go out*, D thought, *but not usually by themselves. They have to be extinguished. A fire can leap and jump and scorch everything in sight. That's why there are fire departments. Someone has to quell the flames. Someone has to face the heat.*

Many ignorant people voted for Trump. Many complacent people didn't for Hillary. Contemporary American history could be boiled down to very simple sentences. The night Trump was elected, D knew what was going to happen. He had spent too many nights watching bullies at nightclubs: sensing weakness, they pounced.

D couldn't let his self-interest cloud his judgment, even if that was the twenty-first-century American way. The contemporary mantra seemed be: *Focus on yourself, ignore the homeless and poor, escape into the digital world*. It was the mind-set that underlined Kurtz's ethos. It had to be addressed—even if the reply came years after the fact. Kurtz and Pilgrim needed their pasts revealed. The comfortable rich needed to feel the cold palpitation when they realized, despite having money, that they were not safe. Insecurity was everywhere in America. The Kurtzes and Amos Pilgrims of the world needed to feel uncomfortable. D stamped out his cigar and went back inside.

Back at his computer, he typed out a list of names and e-mail addresses of folks and websites who wouldn't be afraid: Chuck D, KRS-One, RZA, Spike Lee, Russell Simmons, John Legend, Lauryn Hill, D'Angelo, Immortal Technique, Questlove, Black Thought, Meek Mill, Kendrick Lamar, Ice Cube, Ice-T, Okayplayer, Afropunk, Reverend Al Sharpton, Elliott Wilson, *The Root*, *theGrio*, Anderson .Paak, the *Source*.

He went through Google, made a list of MCs who'd been arrested or convicted during the period Mayer and Jackson had been moles in the hip hop industry. He made a list of community organizations and foundations that addressed mass incarceration and police shootings. He didn't think many in the mainstream media would touch this initially, but he was going to make sure Rachel Maddow, *Politico*, and the *Daily Beast* got an early look. D spent the rest of the evening preparing an introduction to the chapter and a bio of Dwayne Robinson for those unfamiliar with him.

D had no idea if anyone would believe this. The Internet was unde-feated. It could be labeled propaganda. If a real news agency wanted to follow up on it, how could they? He would release the Kurtz video too. That would help. That video, however, was just part of a larger movie.

He'd given Amos Pilgrim a cleaned-up version of the manuscript that absolved him of all agency in the plot against hip hop. But D was going to release the version Ray Ray hadn't doctored, the original that Dwayne Robinson had written raw on his white Apple laptop. Pilgrim was a big boy. Let him stand up and answer all the questions. In other words—fuck him. D pressed send and Robinson's book went out to be read by thousands a decade after it had been written. *I owe you that, my friend*, D thought. *Congrats on its publication.*

CHAPTER FORTY-NINE
BACK TO THE FUTURE (PART II)

D stood stage right almost holding his breath as Night finished the last verse of "White Men in Suits." The crowd at this homeless benefit concert mixed liberal Westsiders, Eastside hipsters, and music fans from all over town. When the crowd's cheers and claps filled the Echoplex, D unclenched his butt cheeks and hugged Night as he came offstage.

He looked over his shoulder at Maggie and the other volunteers thanking Night for performing. D's mind was onto the next act. Tayris's DJ was already onstage, spinning the instrumental to a spacey trap track. Tayris walked over next to D. The young performer's hair was in red-tipped twists, and his red, white, and black jacket hung loose on his shoulders, over his tat-covered torso. D instructed, "Make this your crowd." Tayris nodded and hit her stage.

Tayris Smooth, the waiter from the Four Seasons, had transitioned from a polite server to a swaggering, jumping, "nigga"-spouting, twenty-first-century rapper. To D's ears, the chorus was a bit choppy, with words popping out of incomprehensible sentences. *Bag* was a recurring word, which was easy to translate—bag equals money, money equals cars and women and status. It was a most American sentiment, one the president would have concurred with. Tayris and the balding president shared a value system: *Cash rules everything around me*. Though separated by age, looks, and race, the kid rapper and #45 had a very basic vision of success. The big difference between the Tayris and the #45 was that Tayris was honest about his desires.

Trump, who'd been bankrupt and had sold his soul to Arab oil and Russian dictators, knew that survival was predicated on false honesty and outright lies, ones he told the world and ones he told himself. Trump's boastful declarations were as ridiculous as those of any kid rocking a mic. Boasts were his shield and, crazy as they were, he knew his audacity won him converts. For a people addicted to the sound and fury of reality TV, social media trolling was the greatest form of entertainment.

At one point Tayris started a "Fuck Trump!" chant, which was picked up enthusiastically by the crowd. Ten minutes later, when he was tossing one-dollar bills into the crowd, there was a frenzy to scoop them up, as if the attendees had turned into strippers. *Fuck Trump. Grab money. Trap music.* All parts of the American way.

D glanced over at Maggie, who was a little taken aback by Tayris, but her boyfriend, the handsome white man D had seen with her at the yoga studio, was loving it.

After his set, Tayris came over and asked, "So you saw what I do. You down to manage me now?"

"I love your energy and you have stage presence," D said, "but I'm not sure I understand your music enough to guide you."

"I got that. But you understand how to make money. That's what I need to know."

Against his better judgment, D heard himself reply, "Yes. I know how to do that."

Excerpt from *The Plot Against Hip Hop* by Dwayne Robinson (2011):

Hip hop once felt like a movement, and any movement is defined by its enemies and its ideas. Back in the day, hip hop's enemies were legion: major record labels that didn't believe, R&B and jazz musicians who argued that it dumbed down the culture, booking agents who turned their noses up, venues that didn't want "those people" in their building. Radio stations that made Chuck D question their blackness. Upper- and middle-class blacks who saw it as a threat to their advancement. Black women who hated its use of "bitch." White gatekeepers intimidated by its cultural power, and rockers who saw their dominance over teen rebellion snatched away. Politicians and reverends for whom it was vehicle to raise their status and donations.

This was a grand coalition of opposition arrayed to stop this abomination from degrading our nation. And, of course, they failed. Despite Moral Majority disrespect, music industry disregard, and black adult disdain, hip hop could not be stopped. Black kids and white kids, Asian and Latinos, and all the folks in between found solace, inspiration, vision, voice, identity, home, and even God in its beats, rhymes, dances, slang, clothes, sneakers, and technology, reinventing themselves and hip hop year upon year.

Hip hop was powerful propaganda for the innovation, spirit, and mastery of black American culture, as its emphasis on adaptability and improvisation conquered the globe. It was a profound, unexpected victory that was spawned under presidents Ford and Carter, went national under Reagan, and blossomed under both Bushes and

Clinton. But was the victory the real deal, or was it a fugazi? Was it a real social and economic movement, or just a sepia-toned brand of merciless capitalism? To be continued.

THE END

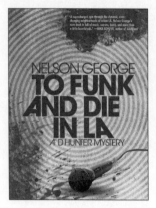

TO FUNK AND DIE IN LA
280 pages, trade paperback, $15.95

"*To Funk and Die in LA* is a supercharged spin through the dynamic, ever-changing neighborhoods of urban LA. Nelson George's new book is full of music, secrets, heart, and more than a little heartbreak."
—Nina Revoyr, author of *Southland*

"A must-read!"
—*BookRiot*

"Ex-bodyguard D Hunter travels from Brooklyn to Los Angeles to investigate the circumstances surrounding his grandfather's murder . . . read this for its passionate and unresolved argument about the still-beating heart of R&B."
—*Kirkus Reviews*

THE LOST TREASURES OF R&B
192 pages, trade paperback, $15.95

"This is a fine mystery and D Hunter is as world weary, yet steadfast, as Philip Marloew, Spenser, Dave Robicheaux, or Easy Rawlins."
—*Library Journal* (Starred Review, Pick of the Month)

"*The Lost Treasures of R&B* is a modern noir thriller, doused in killer beats and Brooklyn cool."
—Shawn Ryan, creator of *The Shield* (TV show)

"Nelson George has created a niche: the incredibly entertaining street-savvy mystery. Add in a passion for Brooklyn and musical greats past and present, and you have a mesmerizing book."
—Allen Hughes, film director, *Menace II Society* and *American Pimp*

THE PLOT AGAINST HIP HOP
176 pages, trade paperback original, $15.95

Finalist for the 2012 NAACP Image Award in Literature

"Wickedly entertaining." —*Kirkus Reviews*

"A carefully plotted crime novel peopled by believable characters and real-life hip-hop personalities." —*Booklist*

"Part procedural murder mystery, part conspiracy-theory manifesto, Nelson George's *The Plot Against Hip Hop* reads like the PTSD fever dream of a renegade who's done several tours of duty in the trenches." —*Time Out New York*

"George's prose sparkles with an effortless humanity, bringing his characters to life in a way that seems true and beautiful." —*Shelf Awareness*

THE ACCIDENTAL HUNTER
216 pages, trade paperback, $16.95

"Great reading for the criminal-minded." —*Vibe*

"Nelson George's smooth security-guard-turned-detective, a.k.a. D, scours a demimonde as glamorous as Chandler's Los Angeles . . . D Hunter definitely needs an encore—he's destined to become a classic." —Mary Karr, author of *The Liars' Club*

"The most accomplished black music critic of his generation." —*Washington Post Book World*